Get ready for the craziest Christmas story EVER!

Perfect for fans of funny fiction

Can Ben save Christmas?

Packed with helicopter chases, daring present deliveries, and tough-talking elves

# WHAT'S INSIDE Santa's emergency briefcase?

James Bond would be jealous of this secret stash of passports and cash. Strictly for use in crash-landings and other sticky situations.

Declan O'Reilly
336-23498-4479-64

USA
JAPAN
China
FRANCE

To Lizzie—my fantastic designer.
Thanks for all your hard work.

# OXFORD
## UNIVERSITY PRESS

Great Clarendon Street, Oxford OX2 6DP

Oxford University Press is a department of the University of Oxford.
It furthers the University's objective of excellence in research, scholarship,
and education by publishing worldwide. Oxford is a registered trade mark of
Oxford University Press in the UK and in certain other countries

First published 2017

British Library Cataloguing in Publication Data

Data available

ISBN: 978-0-19-275896-5

1 3 5 7 9 10 8 6 4 2

Printed in Great Britain
Paper used in the production of this book is a natural,
recyclable product made from wood grown in sustainable forests.
The manufacturing process conforms to the environmental
regulations of the country of origin.

# THE Accidental...
# FATHER CHRISTMAS

Written and illustrated by
## Tom McLaughlin

**OXFORD**
UNIVERSITY PRESS

# LAST CHRISTMAS

Ben took a deep breath and the iciness of the air made his chest tickle. He strode into the department store and up to the entrance of the grotto. Stepping forward, he introduced himself with a quiet nervousness.

'Hi, my name's Ben and I'm thirteen years old.'

Two huge hands came forward and ruffled Ben's hair. He closed his eyes as he felt the soft sheepskin mittens pulling him closer towards that famous red coat.

'Well, Ben, it's nice to meet you. I'm Santa Claus.

Now what can I do for you?'

'Are you the real Santa?' Ben asked, giving the man with the white beard a hard stare.

'Ho ho ho . . .!' Santa smiled. 'Of course . . .'

'It's just there's a man outside who says he's the real Santa too,' Ben pressed him.

Santa peered out of the window and sure enough, there was another Santa ringing a bell and waving to the kids. 'Bill . . .' Santa sighed under his breath. 'Santa has many helpers, in many different places, to make sure everyone's being good.'

'Hmm, well, okay, good answer I suppose. Did you get my letters?' Ben asked.

'Of course I did, ' Santa chuckled.

'Then you know I only want one thing . . .' Ben sighed.

'Was it an egg box?' Santa smiled at Ben.

'A what?'

Suddenly an elf, a suspiciously tall elf, sidled over and whispered something into Santa's ear.

'I mean an Xbox,' Santa quickly corrected himself.

'Errm, no, I have one of those,' Ben said frowning.

'I meant a Play . . . station?' Santa asked, looking at the elf, who nodded sagely.

'No, I have two of those,' Ben huffed. 'You did get my letter?'

'Yes, yes,' Santa sighed impatiently. 'ipad?'

'Nope . . .'

'ipod?'

'Nah . . .'

'iphone?'

Ben shook his head.

'I . . . patch?' Santa said hopefully.

'What?!' Ben replied, feeling really confused.

'A robodrone T-Rex . . .?'

'No, but what's that?' Ben asked excitedly.

'Well, I dunno, I just made it up. Something with lasers probably. Kids love lasers.' Santa shrugged. Ben looked at the elf, who now had his head in his hands.

'Listen, you did *get* my letters, didn't you?!' Ben said, moving closer.

'Arrgh!' Santa yelled, 'My toe! I've got a bunion, I'm not supposed to put any pressure on it.'

'Oh sorry!' Ben winced.

'It's got to come off! The boot and the sock too.'

'OK—erm—back to my letters, did you get them? I have copies right here if you need reminding,' Ben said, pulling some paper from his jacket pocket.

'Oh right, we're really doing this are we?' Father Christmas said, pulling his lumpy foot out of his boot and peeling off his sock.

'November 20th, five years ago. The writing is a little childish and as for the spelling, well, just don't judge:

"Deer Farter kristmas,
Please can Daddy ~~com~~ come
home. I mizz him."

'I have one here from two years ago:

"Dear Santa, I'm not sure if you got my last letter, but still no Dad. Pull your socks up. Love Ben".'

'Yes all right, I've been in these boots all day. Just let me air my bunion before I pull my socks up,' Santa said, waving his foot around.

'No, the sock thing was in the letter, but never mind, I have last year's here too,' Ben said, riffling through his paperwork.

'Your son has a lot of energy!' Santa said, smiling over at Ben's mum, who was waiting at the entrance to the grotto. 'It must be exhausting.'

'Yes, yes it is,' Mum smiled, turning pink with embarrassment.

'Back to my correspondence, this from last June . . . I wanted to make sure it got there in plenty of time:

"Dear So-Called Father Christmas, I notice that once again you haven't delivered on your promise to help my Dad come home for Christmas. He's always working and he says this is his busiest time. Please do this one thing for me or I'll call the police. PS—I won't really call the police, but I just thought I'd put the wind up you."'

'Well Santa does his best, but sometimes he can't make everyone happy. I wish I could,' Father Christmas smiled, putting his sock and boot back on.

'I know I have no right to get any special treatment, but the one thing I want I never get, and you don't seem to know what I'm talking about, so I ask you once again, Santa, are you in fact him? Are you the real Father Christmas?'

By now all the other children in the queue were staring at Father Christmas, waiting for his answer. Ben's mum was grinning but it was a really weird grin. The last time Ben saw that grin was when she threw her famous New Year's Eve party a few years ago and she caught Mr Jenkins from down the road wearing her shoes and lipstick. Mum stopped throwing New Year's parties after that.

'Right, that's it!' the elf said, pulling a rope across the rest of the queue. 'Show's over! We've got a Code Red again, Tina, a kid's asking awkward questions! Last time this happened they threw eggs at Santa. Whatever happened to the magic of Christmas?!'

'I think we should go,' Ben's mum said, grabbing him by the hand and dragging him away.

'But he didn't answer my question!'

'Listen, I'm sure you'll have a bumper stocking full of presents as usual, Ben.' Mum was beginning to lose her patience. 'You always do!'

'That's not what I want! I only ever want the same thing,' Ben sighed. 'I just want Dad to be home for one Christmas.'

'Oh Ben . . . ' Mum stopped in her tracks. 'Look, your Dad loves you very much, but you know how things are. Your Dad is very busy. He works very hard to have the things we like. Expensive Christmases are . . . well . . . expensive. That doesn't mean he doesn't care for us, it just means he has to work hard so that we have everything.'

'I know.' Ben felt embarrassed. 'You don't have to keep telling me, it would just be nice if he was at home for once.'

'Well, maybe next year . . . Now, what say I buy you one of those expensive hot chocolates, with all the marshmallows and frothy cream things with extra syrupy nonsense on?' Mum said kindly.

'Sure,' Ben smiled. He knew they were just pretending that everything was OK but he didn't want to upset Mum. It wasn't her fault. Dad was just very important and had to do important things. But Christmas isn't much fun when you have to play *Guess Who* by yourself because Mum's busy cooking a turkey dinner for two. It was no one's fault really, but that didn't mean it didn't sting.

Mum squeezed Ben tightly as they walked down the bustling high street towards the coffee shop. The other Santa was still ringing his bell and holding out a bucket for people to put change in. Ben felt like he was being lied to—which one was real, or was it neither of them? This wasn't the first time he'd questioned if Santa was real—he'd been having doubts for some time now. It wasn't just the fact that he'd written to Santa so many times and his letters kept getting ignored, but it was other stuff too. Whenever he met Santa in the shops or out and about, the beards didn't look right. Sometimes Santa would have leather boots on, sometimes boring work shoes, and they had funny voices too—one had sounded like his Uncle Cyril from Dudley. Maybe Santa really was from Dudley?

Ben found an empty table while his mum went to get two huge hot chocolates. He reached into his pocket and pulled out his secret notebook. Everyone should have a secret notebook, trust me. Ben opened the page marked 'Evidence that Father Christmas isn't real'. It was a page filled with lots of notes. Like a detective solving a case, Ben had been collecting many clues. He wrote today's date, December 24th, and next to it:

> December 24th
>
> I saw Santa today. He didn't remember
> me or my letters. He also was a little bit
> weird and his feet smelled really badly of
> cheese. I think he's an IMPOSTER!

Ben wrote 'imposter' in really big letters.

Just then Mum came back and plonked the hot drinks down.

'What's that, Ben?' she asked, peering at his notebook.

Ben managed to slip it under the table and into his jacket pocket before she had a chance to read it. 'Nothing,' Ben smiled. 'Sorry about earlier, I didn't mean to sound ungrateful.'

'What are we going to do with you?!' Mum said, ruffling his hair. 'The important thing is that when

Dad is home we get to show him how much we miss him. Some children don't have a dad at all.'

'Like my friend Danny,' Ben added.

'Yes, like Danny.'

 'Or Billy.'

'Well, that's different,' Mum said, her face looking serious. 'Billy's dad is in prison. Robbing a petrol station is very serious.'

'Yeah, I suppose . . .' Ben nodded.

Suddenly their conversation was interrupted by the café owner.

'Time to go home, everyone, we're closing. Have a Merry Christmas, one and all!' the tall man in the apron yelled happily. Even he was wearing a Santa's hat. The man began to close the doors and  flipped the *open/closed* sign over, before standing on a chair, fiddling with a tiny camera in the corner.

'What's that?' Ben asked.

 The owner looked over his shoulder at Ben and smiled. 'It's a camera. You know, in case of burglars, but I think even they get a holiday at Christmas,' he said grinning. 'It takes their picture if they ever try to get in and steal my cookies.'

'Ohh . . .' Ben nodded.

'And if the camera doesn't get them, the trip-wire and trapdoor will!' the man joked.

'Trip-wires and trapdoors,' Ben laughed under his breath. 'Trip-wires . . .' Ben said again.

'I was joking, kid.' The owner smiled nervously. 'I don't really have any of that malarkey.'

Ben broke out into a wide grin, his eyes sparkling. 'Mum, we have to go now! Trip-wires and trapdoors,' he muttered again. That was it— this time tomorrow Ben would know if Father Christmas was real, once and for all.

# DO YOU HEAR WHAT I HEAR?

en rushed through his front door at breakneck speed. He had work to do. He ran upstairs to his bedroom, opened the drawer of his homework desk, and pulled out a piece of paper and his special pen. First he scribbled the layout of the downstairs living room and fireplace, and grabbing a green crayon, filled in the Christmas tree.

This was the plan: everyone knows that Father Christmas's preferred choice of entry is the chimney, so Ben was going to set a trap; we're talking trip-wires, alarms, and cameras. If Santa was real he'd catch him in the act of bringing presents, and he'd ask him a few searching questions about why he hadn't appeared to answer Ben's letters. Maybe Ben would get a selfie, Santa would go on his way, and Ben would have proof and an answer to his letters, and everyone would be happy.

Ben's mum had given Ben her old Polaroid camera. It had a big chunky button and when you pressed this, not only did it take a picture, but the photo popped out of the front of the camera from a tiny letter-box opening. Ben had a few boxes of old film and—as long as he promised no more bottom selfies—he was allowed to use it whenever he liked.

'I'm going to bed now, love. Merry Christmas and I'll see you tomorrow. Don't forget Dad's going to call in the morning!' Mum said, poking her head round the door. Ben quickly sat on his desk, hiding his genius plan. She probably wouldn't approve of his plan to trap and capture Santa like he was a wild rabbit. Mums can be old-fashioned that way.

'Goodnight!' Ben chirpily replied.

'Well someone's cheered up. Why are you sat on

your desk with that camera? Wait, you're not, are you? Ben we talked about this, bottoms are for keeping in trousers, not for showing to Grandmas "who might need cheering up". She is very old and confused. I had to pretend it was a picture of a peach, I'd taken down the supermarket. She thought I'd gone mad.'

'No, no, no, it's not that I promise, I was just having a tidy, you know, got to keep on Santa's nice list,' Ben grinned.

'Hmmm, well OK, it's time for your bed now,' Mum sighed suspiciously.

'Okey-dokes. I shall get my PJs on now.'

Why is it when you want your mum to leave the room they always seem to take ages to go? Ben tried yelling 'pleasegonow!' over and over in his head, but sadly it didn't work.

'Brush your teeth, wash your face with a flannel, and snuggle down. You look like a boy up to shenanigans, and I don't want any shenanigans. I have a no-shenanigans policy round here.'

'No shenanigans,' Ben promised. He had no idea what shenanigans were but he knew that his mother wasn't a fan. And with that she shut the door. Ben quickly went over to the wardrobe next to his bed and opened it quietly. At the bottom, beneath where all his clothes hung in neat rows, was his bric-a-brac box. It was the place where Ben put his collection of interesting things, from bicycle bells to old balls of string, shiny nuts and bolts that caught his eye on the street, to old, broken watches. Ben searched and dug around in it as silently as he could, sourcing all the things he needed for his excellent plan. And then all he had to do was wait.

Half an hour later, the entire house was in darkness. Mum was away to her bed and Ben was in his pyjamas. Pulling his dressing gown off its hook he grabbed the camera, the ball of string, and several old bike cogs, and set about sneaking off downstairs.

'It's on, it's on like Donkey Kong,' Ben said under his breath. He opened the door and tiptoed past his mum's room. Ben smiled to himself. 'This is what I do . . .' he muttered over and over under his breath.

Ben considered himself one of life's great sneakers. He was well used to the odd midnight sneak for milk, and yes, the occasional biscuit. He sneaked at school, particularly on the football pitch where he perfected the practice of moving around without anyone noticing him and therefore avoided having to deal with the inconvenience of a team mate passing him the ball. He occasionally sneaked past whole troops of dinner ladies in an attempt to get out of the biting wind at playtime. His record was magnificent; 458 sneaks for zero catches. Ben headed along the hall slowly, thus avoiding any unnecessary squeaking (which is like kryptonite to sneakers) and began to slink downstairs. This was the most dangerous part of the operation—the stairs. If Ben were to get caught, this would be the most likely place. Anywhere else, there's a cupboard to hide in, or a sofa to leap behind, but on the stairs there was nowhere to go, except straight to the land of Trouble and its capital city, Groundsville.

'Keep calm, keep calm. I am the king. I AM THE KING,' Ben sang, to the theme tune of James Bond, over and over in his head. Ben cleverly placed one foot on the edge of the stair and walked slowly down the edge. The middles of steps could be a bit worn and prone to noise, so by walking down the sides Ben was giving himself the best chance of avoiding capture by the evil Mumzoid. Ben often pretended he was avoiding an army of robot Mums—it gave the whole sneaking around thing a much better sense of adventure. Within seconds, Ben was down and about to enter the living room.

'What's this?' Ben said, looking at the door. 'It's already open, oh this is too easy!'

Ben slithered in through the gap in the door and took a deep breath before carrying on with the next part of the operation. The living room was huge; in fact the whole house was huge. It was fair to say Ben had it good, the best of everything in many ways. He didn't really know what his Dad did, but it paid well. Whenever he had asked, his Dad would always say, 'Oh it's far too boring,' or 'Oh let's not talk about work, let's get the telescope out,' or something. He always seemed distracted. Was his job something to do with numbers, or someone else had some numbers and Dad's job was to check them, or was it money, or both? Ben really had no idea.

He looked over at the Christmas tree—it was probably the tallest one they'd ever had. There's something about a Christmas tree sat in the dark that makes it feel extra magical. A few presents already lay underneath. There was a squidgy one from his nan, which was a jumper. Ben always got jumpers from his nan. They were strange colours, with odd shapes on. Ben had never seen anything like them in the shops so he concluded that it must be a special secret shop where only nans are allowed in. He even got one that fitted him a couple of Christmases ago. It was a shame it was in brown, white, and blue—he looked like a giant bottle of HP sauce. There were some presents from Ben to his mum and dad—chocolates for Mum and aftershave for Dad, called *Momentum*. It was 'for the man who wants it all' and it came free with a glossy magazine about cars. Ben got the magazine and Dad got the aftershave, for when he's home next. Winner!

'Righty-ho,' Ben whispered. 'Let's do this.' He reached into his dressing-gown pocket and pulled out the ball of string. He went over to the fire, which was long extinguished, and he began to tie and weave.

'If I lay some string across the fire place and tie it to the Christmas tree, anyone coming in through the chimney will pull on the string. The bells will jingle on the tree and wake me up. I. Am. A. Genius.' Ben smiled confidently. By the time he'd finished, the front room looked like a giant spider had broken in and left the most ginormous web. Every branch and table leg had string woven around it. Ben shivered thinking about the imaginary giant spider. Ben didn't like spiders; he had a natural distrust of anything that had more legs than him.

Ben hid behind the sofa and waited. He looked at his watch—it was nearly 10 p.m. There was just one thing to do—stay awake!

Ben had no idea how long he'd closed his eyes for, but the sound of his own snoring woke him up. For a second he didn't know where he was, and then he heard something. A faint jingle. Ben looked to the top of the tree and noticed it was swaying—not by much, but enough for him to know this was it.

Silently, Ben sat up and grabbed the Polaroid camera from around his neck, and on his hands and knees began to crawl across the floor. He could feel his heartbeat pounding in his chest. Ben put his hands on the sofa and eased himself round. He lifted his head up and took a look. There was definitely someone there. He saw a shadow, but the Christmas tree was in the way. Ben felt the plastic of the camera as he gripped it tightly. The leather strap was digging into his neck. He knew that he probably only had one chance to get proof, real proof that the most famous man in the world was real and in his house.

Ben felt a surge of bravery pump through his veins and he jumped to his feet. The shadowy figure turned round, and now Ben was standing up he had a better view. Ben pressed his finger on the button of the camera. Could it be, was it . . . ?

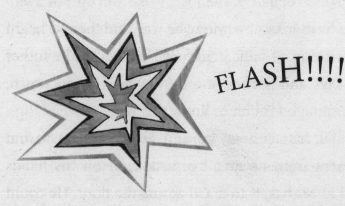

FLASH!!!!

# MUST BE SANTA

or a fraction of a second the room was as bright as the sun, before it was swallowed up by the darkness again. But in that moment, Ben had seen a flash of red and white too.

'Whaaaaaaa!' came a yell. The flash was so bright that Ben was temporarily blinded. There was another scream and the sound of something expensive smashing on the floor. Ben tried to get his bearings, and put his arms out, trying to feel where he was, but he hit the light switch by mistake. Ben didn't move, he just stared. Father Christmas was right there in front of him, looking exactly as you'd expect. He was round in all the right places, with a beard like a snowdrift, and boots that actually looked like boots and not work shoes. It was really him and he was about to fall over. Santa was wrapped up in all of the string. Looking back on it now, Ben supposed that perhaps using 147 feet of string was overdoing it a tad.

'Oh no, don't spin round,' Ben whispered. 'You'll just get caught up more.'

'Arrrgh! Who are you, what's going on?!' Santa cried, desperately trying to untangle his feet.

'If you just calm down and also keep your voice down a bit, you know, stop shouting, that would be really useful.' Ben looked anxiously towards the door, hoping his mum wouldn't wake up and break his sneaking personal best. 'Anyway, I'm Ben. I wrote to you a while back . . .'

'HELP! What's this around my feet?!'

'You're right, this isn't the time or the place. We'll talk about problems with your admin later . . .'

By now Father Christmas was turning round in circles like a hairy spinning top. The more he tried to escape, the more caught-up he got. He made a grab for the bookshelf near the fire to steady himself, but he lost his balance, pulling the bookshelf down with him. Nigella's *Complete Guide to Eating Like a Goddess* was the first to land on Father Christmas's head, followed by *War and Peace*, then several atlases. Ben put his hands over his ears as each new volume made a thick thudding sound as it landed on Santa's head.

The *Guinness World Records*—bam! The complete *Oxford English Dictionary*—thud! *The Encyclopedia of UFOs*—keeeerthwack! Each larger than the last, ricocheting off Santa's shiny dome before the onslaught finally stopped.

'Santa?! SANTA!' Ben yelled. Two things were becoming very clear: firstly, it appeared his mum was the heaviest sleeper in the world, and the sound of a collapsing bookshelf didn't seem to wake her up. Secondly, Santa wasn't moving. Ben ran over to Santa and pulled the books off his face.

'Oh no!' Ben yelled, 'I've killed Father Christmas, oh no, oh no, oh no. This is BAD. They're going to lock me up for ever; I mean who kills Santa? I've literally killed Christmas! Mum's going to go *mental* at me! Wait—maybe there's a way to save him? The kiss of life? It would involve me kissing an old man though . . . Is that worse than letting him die?' Ben mused.

'Neither is great if I'm honest,' Ben continued, throwing himself into the moral dilemma so utterly and completely that he didn't notice Santa's eyes open and roll around in his head.

'Right, pucker up, big guy, I'm going to give you a kiss!' Ben said, grabbing Santa by his beard. At that very second Santa let out a pained groan.

'WHHHAAAAAAAAAA!'

'Wait—you're alive, I don't have to kiss you. I'm so happy I could kiss you!' Ben whooped. Santa moaned loudly again.

'You must have been knocked out, so I need to bring you round. How do I do that?' Ben looked around. 'I know, I'll throw a drink at you. I've seen that on a TV show once; maybe that'll work.'

Ben grabbed a small glass of sweet sherry from the coffee table and hurled it at Santa. It sloshed against his skin as it hit him directly in the nose. Santa just howled again. 'OK, not the result I was hoping for . . . I could slap you. I saw that on a show too; they sort of slapped the person around the face until they woke up. Ben cracked his knuckles, and pulled his arm back, and froze.

'This just feels wrong. I shouldn't really be hitting Santa. 'It's like giving a Chinese burn to a unicorn, it just feels bit wrong,' Ben moaned. 'I know! Smelling stuff; if you smell something really strong, that can wake you up. Smelling salts, I think they call it.'

Ben dashed into the kitchen and looked in the cupboard: pepper, normal salt, no actual smelling salts. Wait, maybe he didn't need smelling salts, just something stinky? Ben had an old sock that he had used to clear up some milk a couple a months ago. It'd been under the bed, he could probably reach it though. But was it powerful enough? Ben looked around the kitchen—there was a jar of pickled onions which would probably work. He could waft an onion under Santa's face, that might bring him round.

Then Ben saw it. It was under a bowl, in a tin, wrapped in foil hidden in a box. It was his Dad's favourite cheese, Old Stinker. He was only allowed it once a year as it 'made the kitchen smell like old man's pants', to quote Ben's mother. It was a cheese so powerful, so potent, that his Dad had put it in the fridge next to a bottle of wine, and it made the wine taste of cheese, without even touching it. Hence having to keep it under several protective layers in the kitchen. Ben edged towards the bowl and lifted the lid. He could already smell it and he was two more layers away. He pulled open the tin foil and started to do his mouth-breathing; it came in very useful when faced with repulsive smells, like cheese and a boy called Lenny Spenk at school who smelled of hot beans. Ben opened the box and there, oozing like a pale snail, sat the cheese. He grabbed a slice and held it at arm's length, heading for Santa. Ben waggled the slice underneath Santa's nostrils.

'Wakey wakey . . .'

Santa's nose wrinkled and snorted, and within a second or two, his eyes opened and he looked down in horror at the cheese.

'Yes, it worked!' Ben cheered.

'Arrrgh, my head. What happened . . . Who are you?' Santa asked.

'Hello, I'm Ben and I would firstly like to say, on behalf of the people of earth, sorry that I may have knocked you out a bit. No harm done, no

need to tell anyone about this and I'm very sorry.
Please don't tell my Mum.'

'Oh,' said Santa. 'I won't! One more question . . .'

'Yes?' Ben smiled.

'Who am I?' Santa blinked.

# BLUE CHRISTMAS

'What?' Ben snapped.

'Who am I?' Santa said calmly.

'You're Santa Claus! You know: St Nick, Father Christmas. You're the man!' Ben said, looking as encouraging as possible. For a second Santa said nothing and then . . .

'HOHOHOHOHOHOHO!' he laughed, I mean belly-laughed, like . . . well, like Santa. 'Oh that's funny, no seriously, who am I and why is my head hurting?'

'You're Santa and I knocked you out . . .

BY ACCIDENT!' Ben quickly added.

'Oh yeah, what are you, an elf?' Santa laughed. 'I think you should get out of my house now.'

'What?'

'You heard. I'd like you both to leave.'

'Both?' Ben said looking round.

Santa's eyes had begun rolling around in his head. He must have been seeing double. 'Yes, both go away. I have something very important I should be doing. If only I could remember what.'

'Oh no,' Ben sighed. 'I've broken Santa Claus. Well this is just perfect, isn't it? I'm definitely going to go to prison for this.'

'Am I supposed to be hairdresser-ing or am I opening the batting for England . . .' Santa mused.

'NO. YOU'RE DELIVERING PRESENTS. YOU ARE FATHER CHRISTMAS,' Ben shouted, before remembering that his mum was upstairs.

'Father Christmas!' Santa laughed. 'There's no such thing!' he chuckled.

'What?! Look at how you're dressed. What's that you're wearing?' Ben pleaded, 'You even have a sack full of presents!'

'That's it!' Santa shrieked.

'At last,' Ben smiled.

'I was on my way to a fancy dress party, obviously.' Santa sniffed, standing up unsteadily, and putting his hands in his pockets defiantly.

'Look!' he said pulling a piece of paper out of his pocket. 'Here's the address. Now listen here, young elf person, I'm off to my Christmas party and you are not going to stop me!'

Santa grabbed a vase filled with flowers from the mantelpiece and wobbled off towards the front door. 'I'll take this as a present. Now I thought I told you to leave!'

Santa stopped for a second. 'I think I have a job to do first.'

'Yes, YES! You do have a job to do.'

'It's all coming back to me now,' Santa said, smiling vacantly. 'I have boots and a bag,' he said, looking around.

'Yes, yes you do!' Ben beamed.

'I work on the bins.'

'No, no you don't!' Ben snapped.

'I am a dustman, I wear a dustman's hat. Now where did I put my "cor blimey" trousers?' Santa asked, looking around. 'Probably in the washing machine . . .' Santa marched off into the kitchen.

'Maybe I should call a doctor,' Ben said under his breath.

'Good idea!' Santa said, tapping his nose. 'It might help that headache of yours.'

'I don't have a headache. I think you might though!'

'I have found my trousers,' Santa sighed with relief. 'You two can stop looking now.'

'Noo! That's my mum's nightie!' Ben waved his arms frantically as he watched the very old, fat man try to put on a silk nightie over his boots and clothes. 'I don't think it's your colour!'

'Nonsense, I feel like a natural woman,' Santa smiled, turning round with the nightie on backwards and upside down.

'Would you like a sit down? I really think you should take a moment,' Ben begged.

'I can't remember if I can juggle knives or not?' Father Christmas asked out loud, to no one in particular.

'Oh please don't, not the knives!'

Santa grabbed a handful from the block on the side, and threw them high into the air. They smashed into the ceiling, some sticking in the plaster, others crashing down all around. 'No, apparently I can't. Anyway, I'm hungry. Who fancies Lamb Bhuna? I'm going to need some lamb and some bhunas; do you have any?'

'No!' Ben cried out in desperation, walking round trying to collect all the knives from the floor. 'Just have a sit down and a glass of water, and we can work it out.'

'Fine,' Santa huffed, throwing the flowers out of

the vase and swigging the cloudy water. 'This coffee tastes off.'

'Oh please don't tell me you actually drank that?' Ben said, looking at the empty vase.

'I have to go. I don't care for your hospitality at all,' Santa said, throwing down a handful of coins.

# 'YOU, SIR, SMELL OF CHEESE!!!'

'No!' Ben pleaded. 'Don't go!' He chased Santa down the hall towards the front door, grabbing a Christmas card as he went. 'Look, this is you! Please believe me!'

'Don't be ridiculous, I'm not a reindeer, I am a HUUUUUMAN! Now leave me be, I'm off to a party with my wife. I forget her name, but she has a splendid hat, very shiny.'

And with that, he was out of the door.

'Wife? What?!' Ben turned round and grabbed the piece of paper that Santa had been waving about. It wasn't a party invitation, it was his delivery list! Ben looked at it more closely.

DELIVERY LIST

2,486 The Queen, Buckingham Palace

2,487 Tom Smith, Fisher Lane

'Buckingham Palace!' Ben gasped. 'He thinks he lives at the palace and the Queen is his wife . . .! Santa, no!' Ben turned and yelled at the door, but it was too late, Santa was disappearing up the garden path. Ben grabbed his shoes, plonked them on his feet and ran out into the night just in time to see Santa hopping on the number 73 bus. This was turning out to be a really horrible Christmas Eve. Ben's bike was in the garage—he'd never get it out in time, let alone keep up with the bus. He could run after it, but really Ben didn't stand a chance.

'Great, this is just great. Santa thinks he's a binman and he's married to the Queen.'

Ben was just about to run upstairs and wake his mum up when he looked at the Christmas card again.

'Reindeer,' Ben whispered. 'Wherever Santa goes, he takes reindeer!'

# SILENT NIGHT

Ben crept upstairs, although why he was bothering to creep he wasn't sure, since his mum was snoring like a traction engine in her bedroom. Ben could have marched up and down the stairs, banging a trumpet, singing 'I've got a lovely bunch of coconuts', and Mum would have still slept like a baby. Ben strode past his bedroom, towards the stairs leading to the attic. He creaked open the door to the attic, which was dusty and smelt of sawdust. Ben walked over to the window and gave it a heave. It clunked open and Ben felt the cold night air hit his lungs.

He looked out over the city, towards the centre, where the number 73 bus was headed. Snow was beginning to fall and he felt a tickle as a snowflake landed on his cheek before turning to water. Ben looked around the attic—it was the place where all the odds and ends were kept, including rugs that were meant to stop paint splattering down and landing on the carpet. Ben grabbed one of these rugs to keep him warm before climbing out of the window. Pulling himself up he looked down and gulped; it was really high. Ben climbed out on to the top of the roof, praying that there would be reindeer up there. He craned his neck and peered over to the main flat part that covered the rest of the house, and then suddenly, without warning, Ben's face was covered in slimy gloop. Was it a cough or a sneeze, or a bit of both? Ben was repulsed and relieved at the same time. He scraped the gloop off his face and opened his eyes to see a real live reindeer inches away, with several others harnessed to a sleigh, behind. Ben couldn't believe his eyes. It was really happening, it was all true.

'Good lad, that's it, don't be alarmed. I'm Ben.'
He wasn't quite sure whether he was expecting the
reindeer to talk back, but he wouldn't have been
surprised. I mean, this was turning into a pretty
weird day, who knew what might happen. Ben
stroked the reindeer's nose and let him sniff his
hand; he knew it was the polite thing to do.

Ben looked at all the reindeer. It was just like the
song—Prancer, Dancer, Cupid, Simon, Chancer—
well, Ben couldn't remember all of them, it was a long
song. There, at the front, must have been Rudolph.

Ben patted him on the snout. Rudolph's nose glowed every time he stroked him. Ben smiled a very big smile. All the reindeer were attached with beautiful red leather reins to a sleigh, bright and shiny red like a fire engine. It had long snow skis for landing, the front seat was dark plum velvet, there were lights and buttons of all shapes and colours on the dashboard, and, in the back, a patchwork sack with the biggest bag of presents Ben had ever seen. The bag was fastened down with rope, so that they wouldn't fall as the sleigh made its way around the world.

'Right lads, listen up! Your boss has gone missing and we need to catch him.' Ben's heart was beating like a bass drum. 'Now, I'll level with you, I've never flown one of these things, so you're going to have to help me out.'

Ben had no idea if the reindeer could understand him, but it felt as though they were listening. He sidled over to the front seat and got in. *Does this thing have a key? Maybe there's a button that says 'Go'.* Ben looked around, but no such luck.

'Oh come on now, how does this thing work?' Ben said, trying to get clues from all the many knobs that peppered the dashboard.

'Does this thing fly on pixie dust?' Ben said, looking in the glovebox. Yes, that's right, Santa's sleigh has a glovebox too.

'Perhaps it flies on Olly Murs CDs?' Ben said, pulling out a handful of discs. He craned his neck and looked down the road.

'There is a petrol station down there, maybe they'd know? I mean, for all I know it needs unleaded. Or maybe Scotch eggs.' Ben picked up the reins. 'I wonder . . . ' he said, and without even thinking about it, he let out a loud 'YEEEEEEHAAAAAAAAAAW!' And just like that, all the reindeer galloped like dogs out of the traps on race day.

'OH MY HOLEY MOTHER OF CHEESE!' Ben shrieked, as the reindeer hurtled towards the edge of the roof. Without thinking, Ben yanked the reins up, and the sleigh shot into the air like a rocket. Within a couple of seconds his whole street was tiny and getting tinier. He could see for miles.

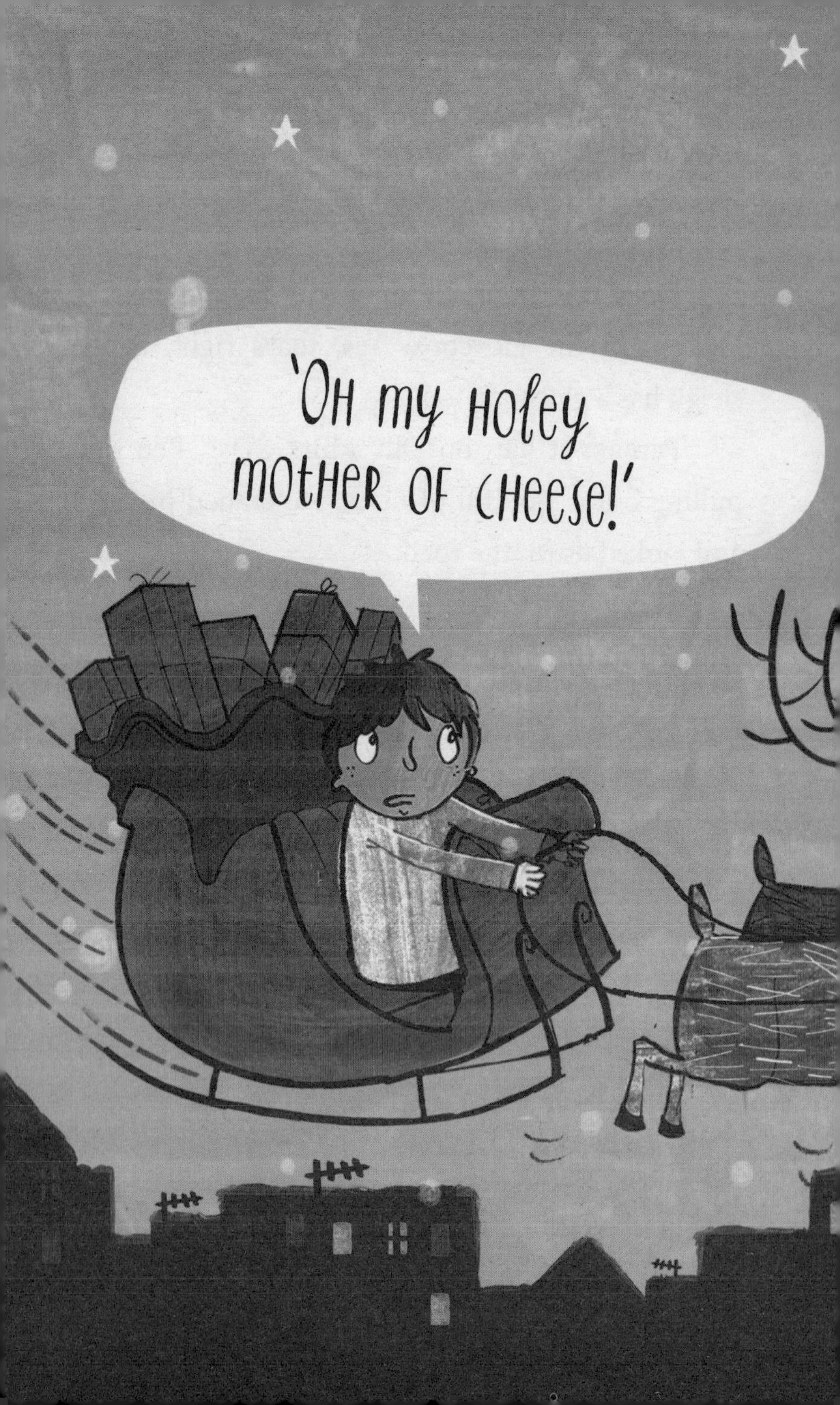
'Oh my holey mother of cheese!'

Well, if he'd managed to keep his eyes open he would have seen for miles. Higher and higher they flew— soon they were the highest thing in the sky, even further into the air than the highest buildings in all of London.

'WHAT'S WRONG WITH YOU?! STOP GOING UP, WE NEED TO GO AFTER THE NUMBER 73 BUS!'

But it was no good, the reindeer weren't listening. Further and further into the sky they flew. Ben was practically vertical, so he was face to face with the clouds. *It must be something to do with these buttons,* he thought, and began to pull and yank all of them at once. Soon the sleigh was twisting and turning in the air, doing barrel roll after barrel roll.

'Oh noooooooo!' Ben cried out in horror as he saw a jumbo jet heading straight for them. He pulled the reins hard left and the many levers too. Thankfully the sleigh avoided the passenger plane by a few feet, in the nick of time. Although Ben was close enough to see the look of horror on the pilot's face as they whizzed past. Ben screamed loudly, diving down back towards the ground.

'Look lads, it's the number 73, down there. Follow that bus!' he cried.

'Ziz iz ze French Airways flight 45639,' the jumbo jet pilot squawked into his radio. 'I'd like to report a UFO over London! This is outraaaageous. I do not expect ze UFOs when I fly. . .Yes, it had flashing lights and a strange creature who appeared to be mouthing "Poooooing heck, we're all going to die". Yes I did say zat correctly, I am excellent at reading ze lips! Zere is a UFO up 'ere and I want it dealt wiz!' the pilot snapped, before hanging up the receiver.

'Did you see that, Pierre?' The pilot shook his head and turned to his co-pilot. 'It is absolutely shocking.'

'I know!' Pierre answered, staring down. 'Look at the size of my little fish. I know the airline meals are small, but this little fish is very little.'

'Oh someone please help me,' the pilot murmured.

Deep in an underground bunker, in a part of the military that most people don't know exists, the phone rang. It was answered straightaway, as though the man was expecting it to ring. The voice was firm, but fierce.

'This is Number 1. A UFO? London? . . . I knew it. It's the same every year, it's always the same. I'm on it. This UFO is mine, ALL MINE! I won't fail this time . . .' he said, slamming the phone down.

# SLEIGH RIDE

In a glamorous part of London, a lady in a posh frock emerged from one of the city's finest eateries, along with her rather rotund husband, and headed out into the night.

'Geoffrey, GEOFFREY!' she bellowed, shattering the peace and quiet.

'Yes, my little piccalilli,' he said wearily.

'Where's the brolly?' she snorted.

'Brolly?' he sighed.

'Yes, the brolly . . .' She looked up into the sky. 'It looks like rain, dear . . .'

Suddenly there was a huge whoosh and roar as Rudolph, Blitzen, and Dave skimmed the tops of their heads.

'Well, you're not wrong!' the man yelled, as he hit the floor with fear.

'Right, here's a safety tip, lads, STAY AWAY FROM ANY PASSENGER PLANES,' Ben howled. 'AND TALL BUILDINGS!' Ben pulled the reins up around his nose. 'I feel sick!' he cried painfully. 'There must be a way to fly this thing properly.' Ben looked frantically at the dashboard and yanked a bright yellow lever. The sleigh flew up and down as Ben moved the lever up and down. 'Bingo!' Ben said, 'That must control the height. OK, what about this red one?' Ben pulled again and suddenly the sleigh slowed right down. Another yank of the lever and pull of the reins and suddenly they were under control. Ben turned round. The back of the sleigh had a rudder like a boat on it, and he realized that if he moved it, he could steer the sleigh like a boat too. That afternoon riding the pedalo in the park last summer wasn't wasted after all. If he could control the left and the right with the rudder, the height with the yellow lever, and the brakes with the red one, he might stand a chance of not crashing. Ben swished and swooped between the church spires and office blocks.

'There's the bus! Right, let's follow it. I'm not letting it out of my sight.'

Along the high street the bus went, zigzagging its way past cyclists and pedestrians, before it headed for the bridge beneath the railway line. There was no room to fly over it as a large skyscraper was in the way, and Ben, being a relative novice at sleigh-piloting, didn't feel confident enough to give it a go.

'Oh great!' Ben said, pulling the reins and the red lever at once. The sleigh made a sharp turn and lurched right, down a side street. 'Don't worry, I know a shortcut that will take us back to the main road.'

The sleigh bounded and bobbed down the side street, knocking over bins and scaring cats all the way, before speeding through a fast food burger drive-thru. Ben slammed on the brakes—perhaps he'd got his shortcuts mixed up? He was suddenly feeling decidedly lost.

'This isn't right. Should I have gone left then right, not right then left, right? Or is that wrong, or is that left? I've got no choice . . .' Ben looked around. 'I need to ask for some directions.'

Ben looked at the dashboard and pressed a purple button. Suddenly a loud horn bellowed out, causing car alarms in several streets to activate.

'Ooowww,' Ben said, holding his ears, 'that's not it—but wow! Let's try this one . . .' Ben pushed in a bright orange button and suddenly the theme tune to *The Archers* blasted out at 100 decibels.

'For the love of cheese!' Ben cried out, hitting it again instantly. 'I guess that's the radio then.' The reindeer mooed and barked in displeasure. 'Sorry, lads.' 'Come on, where are you?' Ben hit a blue button. There were a couple of loud beeps, and then a robotic voice started up with the mantra, 'This sleigh is reversing, this sleigh is reversing . . .'

'Bingo wings!' Ben clenched his fist in delight. Slowly but surely the sleigh reversed back to the drive-thru.

'Right, boys, act natural.' Ben reached out to the button by the side of the drive-thru window and pressed it firmly. There was a ding-dong sound and a spotty teenager who went by the name of Spud, according to the badge on his uniform pocket, opened the window.

'Welcome to Big Max Drive-Thru, home of the Big Max Burger, and Big Max Fries, registered trademark, how can I help you?' he reeled off, in a slightly squeaky teenager's voice, as if he'd said it a thousand times before.

'I just wanted to ask for directions ...' Ben started, but he never managed to finish, as Spud slammed the window shut again.

Ben pressed the button, as before, and the window slid open.

'Welcome to Big Max Drive-Thru, home of the Big Max Burger, and Big Max Fries, register ...' Spud said, completely oblivious to the fact that Ben was parked at a fast food take-away restaurant with several animals and a magic sleigh.

'Yes, I know!' Ben barked, 'I was just here, in fact I

am still here; like I said before I just need directions . . .'

And just as before, the door slid shut.

'I AM GOING TO SCREAM!' Ben screamed. He pressed the button once again.

'Welcome to Big . . . '

'Shut up! I'm not a violent boy, but I'm feeling quite punchy at the moment. Please just talk to me; if I buy something, will you please just talk to me?!'

'Yes,' Spud sighed, 'but you have to buy something. Those are the rules. I don't like them, those are just the rules.'

'I think you do like the rules . . . Right, give me a moment,' Ben said, and once again the window slid shut.

Ben looked in his dressing-gown pocket on the off chance that there might be a few coins in there, but—zero, zilch. Ben felt under the seat. Maybe there was a wallet, or something? He felt something hard and made of leather. Ben gave it a pull and out popped a briefcase. He clicked it open and inside were dozens of passports and envelopes filled with cash. Each passport had a picture of Santa in it, but a different name. In Ireland he was called Declan O'Reilly, in Germany he was called Wolfgang Von Snicklegruuber, and in America he was Chip

Chesterson Jnr III. These must be false passports in case he ever gets lost or crash-lands. It was like something out of a Bond film. But the good news was that Ben now had enough money to buy some food and ask Spud for directions. Ben pressed the button one last time.

'Welcome . . .' Spud stopped, looking at Ben's furious face. 'How may I help you?'

'I'd like a Big Max meal, with a Whammy Jammy

Shake and apple pie, you know one of those ones that's so hot it gives you a suntan just to look at it . . . er . . .' Ben said, looking at the reindeer. 'And seven hundred carrot sticks please.' Dave the reindeer howled. 'All right, all right, make that eight apple pies.'

'Anything else?'

'And a side of directions too, please.' Ben smiled. 'How do I get back to the high street from here?'

'Down the corner and then turn left and right and then left again, and that'll bring you out by the bus depot. I'll get your order,' Spud said, before wandering off.

'That's my good bud, Spud!' Ben smiled.

Two seconds later, Spud opened the window and handed Ben a bag.

'Wow, it took me longer to say than it took you to cook,' Ben said, looking suspiciously into his bag.

'Here's your order, and here are your carrot sticks and apple pies.' Spud handed Ben seventeen bags. 'Merry Christmas and enjoy your meal. Nice reindeer by the way—they almost look real.' Spud sighed, before sliding the shutter across.

Ben grabbed his burger, gave it a bite and with the other hand whipped the reins, and the sleigh shot off in the direction Spud had pointed out. It was amazing to Ben how few people looked up any more. He watched as hundreds of revellers all walked with their heads down, not noticing that only a few feet above their heads was a sleigh flying across London.

'Aha!' Ben could see the bus as they came round the corner back to the main road just as Santa was getting off. He was a five-minute walk from the palace. Ben needed to park somewhere no one would see. He flew high above the street and circled the whole scene. There! Ben saw a quiet park near the palace which was perfect. Ben circled once more and then, with his eyes shut, made his final approach. There was a clang and some caterwauling from several birds, and a crash and a clang as he took the top off a lamp post, but he made it down. Ben grabbed the bags of carrots and split them between the reindeer. 'I'll be back soon, lads. Stay loose and hang tight, or hang loose and stay tight. Oh, you get the idea—don't move. I've got a Santa to catch!'

# LONELY THIS CHRISTMAS

Having best repaired the lamp post (Ben stuck a note on it saying, 'sorry about the lamp post'), he bounded out of the park towards the palace. He flattened down his hair and picked the moths out of it and looked around for Santa. It was getting late now but the streets were still heaving with people. That's the thing about a big city, it never stops; there's always places to go, things to do. It was one of the things Ben loved about it. There was always an adventure to be had, a story to see unfolding before your eyes. I mean, who knows? Perhaps only a mile away there was another kid who was on the hunt for the Easter Bunny, who he'd accidentally injured trying to prove he was real . . .

Ben's eyes scanned the crowd. He didn't want to lose Santa again. Then suddenly he saw him! (Santa that is, not the Easter Bunny.) Ben hurtled through the crowd, pushing, nudging, and apologizing all in equal measure, towards the man in the red hat. He was just about to grab him when the man turned round—it wasn't Santa after all, it was just a man wearing a stupid Christmas hat. Ben's shoulders slumped with disappointment. Ben looked round; it seemed every other person was wearing a Santa hat. How was he ever going to find him now? Then something caught his eye, something out of place. What was it? Ben scanned the palace and its walls. There, in the shadows, was a man was trying to climb up the gates. Not just any man, but Santa Claus! Ben ran over and grabbed hold of Santa's boots.

'What are you doing?' Ben said, trying not to draw any attention to the situation.

'Oh not you again, why are you always

bothering me? I am very old and tired and all I want to do is go and kiss my lady wife.'

'She's not your wife,' Ben said, trying to talk some sense into the man. 'You can't go around kissing the Queen of England. They have laws against that sort of thing.'

'Yes she is. This is our small house and . . . Oh,

I could murder a mince pie, I don't know why . . .
I work as a binman and she looks after the dogs,' Santa
said, pointing at the palace. 'I appear to have forgotten my keys again, so I'm going in over the wall.'

'"Small house"? It's a palace!'

'Well, I wouldn't say palace, but we like it. We
just had it repainted; it makes it look spacious on the
outside, but on the inside it's quite small, you know.'

'What are you talking about?' Ben said, making a
grab for Santa's dangling leg.

'I simply don't know!' Santa grinned
triumphantly.

'You really did hit your head hard, didn't you?'
Ben shook his head.

'My brain feels itchy,' Santa whispered. 'And I can
now taste noises in the air,' he added, before going a
little cross-eyed. 'I have a picture of her.'

'Who?'

'My wife! Look, here she is looking very determined,' Santa said, handing Ben a piece of paper.

'That's a £10 note,' Ben sighed. 'That's not a
picture, and stop kissing it!' Ben cried out.

He glanced round to see a policeman not too far away. Buckingham Palace has lots of police guarding it. They look very scary and some of them even have guns.

'Listen, you have to get down now or bad things will happen!' Ben begged. 'There's a policeman coming . . .'

'Oh good. Ociffer, Ociffer!' Santa shouted, like he was trying to attract a waiter's attention in a busy restaurant.

'This elf. Not elf, I meant *elf* . . . I said "elf" again didn't I? Sorry, I'm getting all my confused words again. What are those creatures called who are as small as elves, but not elves, they get bigger and turn into peoples?'

'Children?' the policeman said, walking over.

'Oh great!' Ben sighed.

'Yes, children, well, Ociffer, this children is trying to steal my trousers,' Santa snapped.

'It's "officer", actually,' the policemen said. 'Yeah, Bravo Delta, we've got another one. Looks like another protester, probably one of those Fathers for Justice people.'

'Now, sir,' the policeman said, addressing Santa. 'Why don't you come down here and we can have a good chat?'

'I like to chat. Why don't you sit on my knee and you can tell me what you want for Christmas, if you like.' Santa smiled.

'What?' the officer said, looking shocked.

'What?' Santa replied. 'I don't know what you want for Christmas, don't ask me.'

'Sir, now don't take this the wrong way, but have you been drinking?' The officer was beginning to lose his patience.

'Ludicrous amounts, Mr Policeman!' Santa grinned back. 'Now give me a leg up, and help me get inside my house!'

'Errr . . . Haha . . .' Ben laughed nervously, trying to keep the peace. 'He doesn't know what he's saying.'

'YOU DON'T LIVE HERE!' the policeman yelled. 'I know everyone who lives here and you're definitely not on the list.'

'Well, check it twice. Everyone should check a list twice . . .' Santa stopped mid-sentence. 'I'm sure

63

there's something I should be doing today.'

'Sorry officer, he's my . . . grandad and he's just a bit confused. Let me take him home,' Ben pleaded. He pulled Santa down and whispered into his ear, 'Now listen to me, we need to get out of here, otherwise this policeman is going to arrest you, and no one wants that, agreed?'

Santa looked at Ben and at the policeman. 'Agreed!' he said tapping his nose.

'Leave him with me, I'll get him home safely,' Ben said, using his bestest, sweetest smile.

'I think that's best. My grandad's the same, gets merry at Christmas and suddenly thinks he's Frank Sinatra. I'll let it go this time, but if he tries to scale the wall of the palace again I'll have to call for back-up, or maybe just shoot him. Now you, young lad, need to get home and back to bed. You don't want to bump into Santa!' the policeman said, pinching Ben's cheek.

'You don't know the half of it,' Ben muttered under his breath. 'Thanks, Mr Officer, we appreciate it, don't we Grandad?'

'Yes we do! Appreciate what?' Santa asked. Ben pulled on Santa's sleeve. 'Come this way, I've got something to show you, Santa.'

'Why do you keep calling me that?'

'Because that's who you are,' Ben snapped, 'and I think I know a way I can prove it.'

# ALL I WANT FOR CHRISTMAS IS YOU

High above London, between the clouds and the shadows, zipped a helicopter, darting between the skyscrapers like an insect looking for prey. The engines were silent and the windows blacked out. This was no ordinary helicopter, because this was no ordinary mission.

'Well, this is lovely. It's nice to get out and about, isn't it? Did you remember to pack a hamper, Number 3?' the pilot asked. The co-pilot reached down between his feet and pulled up a picnic hamper.

'Yay!' he said.

'Yay,' the pilot high-fived back. 'It's like being on a real army mission, isn't it, Number 4?'

'This is a real mission!' a voice boomed from the back of the helicopter.

'Sorry, Number 1,' Number 3 and 4 both replied, like two naughty children.

'Are you all right, sir? Do you want a soothing foot massage?' the last member of the team chipped in.

'That's fine, Number 2. I don't need anyone to touch my feet.' Number 1 was feeling exasperated. 'I just need people to not touch my feet and to not treat this mission as an Easyjet flight to Benidorm.'

Number 3 put down his packet of mini cheddars. 'Where are we off to, Number 1?'

'We are off to solve one of the great mysteries of our time.'

'What happened to white dog poo?' Number 4 asked. 'There was loads of it around when I was a kid. Now you can't find it anywhere, and I know, I've looked.'

'You're weird, Number 4.' Number 3 shook his head.

'No!' Number 1 roared. 'Although, that does remain a total mystery. No, we are going to discover if we are alone in the universe. If there are creatures out there from another world . . .'

'Oh but boss, it's Christmas, if we went home now, we could still catch *The Two Ronnies* Christmas repeat,' Number 3 sighed.

'You two should be ashamed of yourselves, talking to Number 1 like that. I mean, it's not just anyone who gets to fly around in big black helicopters on secret missions, is it?' Number 2 snapped, leaping to Number 1's defence.

'Thank you, Number 2.'

'I mean, look at it, it's a lovely helicopter. It's quiet so no one can hear, it has sat-nav, cupholders . . . You should be a bit more grateful. All this alien stuff is very important to Number 1.'

'Thank you Number 2, yes, yes it is,' Number 1 nodded.

'I mean, most people think he's an idiot for flying around looking for little green men.'

'Wait, what, who says I'm an idiot?'

'Doesn't matter. You pay no attention to them, Number 1. So what if they call you "crazy" and do impressions of you behind your back . . .'

'What, they do impressions of me?!' Number 1 was getting rather alarmed by now.

'Yes, nothing too bad, they dress up as aliens and they sing a song about how they're being chased by Number 1.'

'Wait, there's costumes and a song?! Who does this, the soldiers at the base?!'

'And there's the name,' Number 3 added, unhelpfully.

'My name? What's wrong with my name?' Number 1 asked, his voice full of panic.

'Your name's Number 1, you know . . . ' Number 4 smiled sadly.

'Like wee-wee!' Number 3 added cheerfully.

'Could be worse though.' Everyone looked round at Number 2.

'It doesn't matter whether aliens exist or not. They've given you a shiny helicopter to go and find them, and if that means we have to fly around on Christmas Eve, missing *The Two Ronnies*, then so be it,' Number 2 insisted.

'Well, they totally do exist,' Number 1 huffed. 'I thought the boys back at the base loved to listen to my stories of alien hunting. I didn't realize they were laughing at me,' Number 1 lamented. 'I feel quite upset about the whole thing.'

'Don't worry, sir, tonight's the night, I'm sure,' Number 4 smiled. 'We're about two minutes from landing, from where the last UFO report came from, so try and relax and we'll be there soon.'

'Err, Number 2 . . .?' Number 1 asked.

'Little foot massage?' Number 2 offered.

'That'd be lovely,' Number 1 smiled.

A few, relaxing moments later, the blacked-out X Squadron helicopter was in position.

'It looks awfully high . . .!' Number 2 said, peering

over the edge, his moustache bouncing in the breeze.

'This is what we do,' Number 1 said, grinning.

'Is it?' Number 2's voice wobbled with nerves.

'Yes. That's why we joined up,' Number 1 grinned. 'For moments like this.'

'Not me, I was in the catering division.' Number 2 looked nervous.

'What?! I asked for the best of the best!' Number 1 sighed.

'I am the best of the best. I make the best cottage pie in the kitchen,' Number 2 snapped.

'No, I meant the best of the best at soldiering, not making pie.'

'Oh, I totally didn't get that. But maybe if we catch some aliens, to celebrate I can make us all a pie . . .' Number 2 added hopefully.

'Yeah, all right. Now, after 3, we jump. Hold on to the rope tightly. 1 . . . 2 . . . 3!' With that, the two soldiers hopped out of the helicopter and landed silently in the quiet streets of London, away from prying eyes. They were like ghosts. Well, one ghost and a highly-trained chef. Not because their work was dangerous, but the mere fact that if the public knew they were there, there would be panic on the streets of London. They were experts in tracking down UFOs. You may think people who believe in little green men and flying saucers are crackpots, or maybe you think this kind of thing is only for nerds on the internet, who believe that the moon isn't real and the Queen is really a crocodile in disguise. But high at the top of government, they take everything seriously. There have been so many sightings around this time of year that it can't be coincidence.

'What do we have on the electro-magnetic counter, Number 2?' Number 1 asked, having untied the rope and let it fly off with the helicopter.

'Through the roof, Number 1. The last time we saw something this big was . . .'

'The Milton Keynes incident of 2014,' Number 1 muttered under his breath. 'The greatest unexplained light phenomenon of recent years. We're close, I can feel it in my fingers, I feel it in my toes.'

'Love is all around us!' Number 2 sang. 'Oh, sorry, I thought we were doing a thing . . .' Number 2 looked at his feet, feeling a little embarrassed.

'You don't think, sir . . .' Number 2 started.

'What?' Number 1 asked.

'No, you'll laugh at me . . .'

'No I won't, the army as an organization is obliged to listen to any suggestions. There will be no laughing, sniggering, or sneering,' Number 1 promised.

'Well, these strange lights, we see them every Christmas time; do you think it could be . . .?'

'What? Spit it out!'

'Father Christmas and his magic sleigh, flying through the night?' Number 2 said, a little quiver of excitement causing his voice to shake.

'Father Christmas . . .?!'

'You see, I knew you'd laugh. It sounded reasonable in my head.'

'Father Christmas? Are you ill? You think that this phenomenon, seen all across the world, is a man in a beard with a herd of animals strapped to a toboggan?'

'Well, I mean, is that less likely than aliens?!' Number 2 answered back, before immediately regretting it.

'I've seen these things! Are you saying I'm making it all up?!' Number 1 snorted. 'I'm legally obliged to take any suggestions seriously, as your line manager. There is no such thing as a bad idea, but really, Number 2, you're pushing it. This will go in your appraisal,' Number 1 huffed. 'Father Christmas indeed. I expect a certain amount of sneering from others in the army, I am well aware that most people think that this unit, X Squadron, is a waste of time, but I didn't expect it to come from my own men.'

'Sorry sir, I don't know what I was thinking. Please don't pay any attention. I love the army, it's so cool. I mean, the clothes are great, we get to grow moustaches, and no one laughs at us. Please sir, I'm sorry.'

'All right, all right. Let's park this to one side and get on with our mission, and we can talk about this at our monthly regional team meeting. It's aliens, Number 2, trust me. There's something very odd just round the corner and we're going to stop it, whatever it takes.'

# STOP THE CAVALRY

Santa followed Ben towards the dark corner of Hyde Park where Ben had crash-landed the sleigh. Big Ben chimed half past eleven in the distance. It was getting late—Ben wasn't sure of the maths, but he knew that Santa needed to get going, otherwise a lot of children were going to wake up disappointed.

'Do you remember who you are?' Ben asked hopefully.

'No.' Santa sighed.

Ben waited a couple of seconds. 'What about now?'

'No!'

'Now . . .?'

'NO!' Santa cried.

For a moment there was silence and then Santa looked at Ben. 'I might be called Nigel. Maybe I'm an accountant . . .?' He looked hopeful.

'Oh for goodness' sake. Do you know anything about being an accountant?' Ben puffed out his cheeks in frustration.

'Erm, no.'

'Well, then you're probably not, and before you say anything, you're not called Steve and you don't work as a carpet salesman, nor are you called Julian and you don't work as a dentist, and I'm fairly sure that you're not Timothy the bloomin' ballroom dancer. You, my friend, are Santa. Let's start with the very basics—have you heard of a thing called Christmas? It's when you invite family over that you pretend you like, you eat too much, and if you're over 25 you fall asleep in front of the TV.'

'Yes, I have definitely heard of that.'

'Well, that's a start. There is someone very

important when it comes to Christmas; any ideas?'

'Is it Jesus?'

'There are two people who are very important when it comes to Christmas; there's Jesus, well done for pointing that out, and a chap called Father Christmas. One of them is you. Now I think we can both rule out Jesus, so that leaves Santa,' Ben said, looking at Santa.

'Oh,' Santa sighed, 'when will you leave this alone?'

'Have you seen yourself, man? If you're not Santa, it's a heck of a look you're working there, my friend: beard, rosy cheeks, red suit, black boots, big wobbly belly.'

'Oi, do you mind? Yes, I might be carrying a few extra pounds, but it's winter and we all comfort-eat in winter,' Santa said, grabbing his rather large belly and trying with all his might to heave it in.

Just at that second, a helicopter whizzed overhead, breaking Ben's train of thought. 'That's very low. It's really quiet too.'

'It's probably the police. Perhaps they're looking

for someone,' Santa replied.

'You could be right. We don't want any more close shaves with the police again. We should get out of here. I did tell the policeman that I'd take you home.' Ben suddenly stopped in his tracks. 'That's it, how could I have been so stupid? Home!' Ben grabbed Santa's hand. 'Come on, you're coming with me.'

By the time Ben and Santa got back to the sleigh, it was turning into a tourist attraction. There were people sat on the sleigh, others taking pics with their phone.

'Wow!' a man yelled in a bright American accent. 'He looks like the real deal. Nice costume there, pal,' he said to Santa.

'Actually, he's the real Santa,' Ben interrupted.

'Oops, yep, you got me. He sure is!' the man said, tapping his nose as if he was playing along.

'Oh my, I don't have time for this,' Ben said under his breath.

'Let's play a game. It's called, "let's pretend Ben's right for five minutes"—okay?' Ben whispered.

'Okay,' Santa smiled. 'I like games!'

'Good. Imagine, for some reason, I'm telling the truth and you are Santa. What sort of thing does Santa use to carry out his work?' Ben said, looking at the sleigh.

'A sleigh?' Santa said, getting the hint.

'Yes!' Ben smiled, 'This is good, this is excellent.'

'So, we have a sleigh right here. Now, what's special about Santa's sleigh? It's not any old sleigh, is it?'

'No, it flies,' Santa said, getting into this little quiz.

'Good, this is excellent. So if, say, we got in this sleigh and it flew—could you, would you accept that there's a possibility that I'm telling the truth?' Ben said, nudging him helpfully.

Santa frowned sceptically.

'Uh-uh,' Ben said shaking his head, 'I still have four minutes and thirty seconds left. Come on, let's go.' Ben ushered Santa towards the front of the sleigh.

'What are we doing?' Santa asked.

'You and I are going on a trip,' Ben grinned.

'Where?' Santa looked confused.

'Up there.' Ben looked towards the night sky as he untied the ropes from the tree.

'What?!' Santa looked worried.

'You promised, remember?' Ben smiled.

'Can we get a selfie with Santa?' the tourist asked.

'Okay, okay, everyone in,' Ben said hurriedly, still prepping the sleigh. 'That's it, everyone smile.'

'Your costume is very realistic,' a lady said to Santa as they all stood still waiting for Ben. 'I'm not sure why you've set the sleigh up so out of the way. People aren't going to find you here in the dark. You should park your quaint little tourist thing near the palace or something.'

Santa turned round. 'I'm not allowed near the palace. Apparently there are rules about breaking in

and trying to kiss the Queen.' Santa shrugged.

'Oh my . . . ' the tourist smiled a little nervously.

'And one, two, three!' There was a flash from the camera as everyone smiled. Santa shook his head—the flash had startled him and seemed to bring something back—some far-away distant memory of who he was. He remembered another flash, and how he was somewhere dark, then came pain. Father Christmas tried to remember, but he couldn't piece it together somehow. As quickly as it arrived, the memory was gone again.

'Are you okay?' a man asked Santa. 'You don't look yourself.'

'Myself? I wish I knew who that was,' Santa said in a gloomy fashion.

'Is your Santa all right?' the man asked Ben.

'I feel like I'm from another planet,' Santa added dreamily.

Ben handed the camera back to the tourists and turned to look at Santa closely.

'There was a flash and I felt pain in my head.' Santa looked at Ben, scared that what Ben was saying might actually be true.

'Yes, that's right! I think we need to get you home,' Ben smiled. 'Thanks for the photo, guys, but we've got to fly.'

'Fly . . .' Santa repeated nervously.

'Let's get you in the sleigh and settled down,' Ben said calmly.

'Are you sure he's all right?' the man said, looking at Santa closely.

'We can always ask for some help from those policemen,' the lady said, pointing off into the distance.

Ben squinted into the darkness and could just about make out a couple of men, holding what looked like guns. There was a flash of red laser pointing in Ben and Santa's direction. In the background there was a helicopter, its blades silently whirring round.

'I don't think those are policemen,' Ben said, sitting beside Santa and gripping the reins tightly. 'Those are soldiers, and they're looking for something.'

The men were dressed head to toe in black. It was like trying to watch shadows; one second they were there, then the next they were gone. Ben sensed they were trouble and he knew it was only a matter of time before the soldiers clocked them.

'Well, it's been lovely to meet you. On behalf of the British Tourist Board, thank you and I hope you got some nice pictures and have an enjoyable stay in England. Goodbye now, goodbye, you can go now. Thanks!' Ben hurriedly yelled, before yanking on the reins.

'Oh look, it moves. I wonder what else it does?' the lady said.

Ben yanked on the reins even harder and the sleigh began to pick up speed. He glanced nervously at the soldiers in the distance, and knew it was only a matter of time before they saw the sleigh.

'Hold on,' Ben said firmly to Santa, and with that he pulled the reins back, and like a plane speeding down the runway, the whole sleigh took off into the wind.

Below them, the tourists' mouths opened in wonder.

'Gee, it's so realistic, it's almost as good as Disneyland here. Is that on strings or something?' one lady smiled. 'What, why are you all looking at me funny?'

There was a whoosh and a trail of light as the sleigh flew through the trees and out of the park. Ben looked below as he saw the soldiers start running in their direction. Ben's instinct was right. He didn't know who they were, but they were definitely after him and Father Christmas.

'Number 2!' Number 1 yelled. 'Look!' he said, watching whatever it was zooming between the trees.

'The readings are through the roof!' Number 2 yelled. He pulled out a gun and fired it up at the sleigh. 'It's a GPS tracker; now we can follow them wherever they go.'

The soldiers arrived by the tourists just in time to see the tiny flashing lights disappear into the clouds.

'He said he was from another planet . . .' one man said with astonishment.

'I knew it,' Number 1 smiled to himself. 'I'm bringing this one in. Dead or alive.'

# I'LL BE HOME FOR CHRISTMAS

'Arrrrrgh!!' Santa screamed. 'I'm going to die, you're going to kill me, please stop killing me. AAAAAAAAARGH!!!'

'That was close,' Ben said, turning round.

'Don't turn round, look in front of you!' Santa cried. I mean, he was actually crying by now. 'I want my mummy.'

'Santa, you need to calm down now.'

'MUMMY!! GET ME MY MUMMY!'

'SANTA, IT'S REALLY HARD TO STEER WHEN YOU KEEP SHOUTING!' Ben yelled back.

'Oh great. Now you're sucking your thumb.'

'I don't want to die,' Santa whimpered.

'I don't want to kill you, but unless you stop yelling and shrieking . . .' Ben said crossly.

'What, you're going to kill me?!' Santa sobbed.

'No, that was a joke. A bad one, I'll admit. But you do need to stop crying and shouting—we can't keep this up all the way to the North Pole.'

'Wait, what?'

'The North Pole. I'm taking you home, just like the policeman said. If that doesn't remind you of who you are, I don't know what will,' Ben said. The good news was that the shock of heading to the North Pole had stopped Santa crying at least.

'Are you sure this is a good idea?' Santa asked.

'Look, I can't make you remember who you are. Just telling you you're Santa over and over isn't working—I need some help. I need to take you home. It's the only thing I can think of, so unless you've got any bright ideas, that's where we're going,' Ben said firmly.

'OK, you're the boss.' Santa sat back and made

himself comfortable at last.

'Right, there is just one tiny problem,' Ben said, looking around him.

'What?'

'I don't actually know where the North Pole is. Aha, that's what I've been looking for.' Ben pulled a few levers and yanked on the reins again. 'Hang on, we're going down . . .'

The sleigh swooshed down from the clouds towards a huge roundabout, where it hovered about ten feet above the ground, following the road round.

'Not that one . . . not that one . . .' Ben said, reading the road signs for the different exits.

'What are you doing?' Santa asked, as they flew round and round the roundabout.

'Looking for a sign, and there it is! M1 The North!'

Ben smiled, before sticking his hand out the side of the sleigh to indicate he was turning off the roundabout and up the motorway. A very confused-looking driver slammed on his brakes as the sleigh flew past his window.

'Is your plan to fly following the road?' Santa asked.

'Well yes, I mean this is heading north, towards the pole,' Ben said, smiling as they flew above the traffic.

'All right, all right, say I *am* Santa,' Santa said.

'You are,' Ben replied instantly.

'Say I am, and say I live in the North Pole . . .'

'You do.'

'Say I do. It's hardly going to be at the end of this road. We need to properly work out where it is.'

'Well, do you have any bright ideas?' Ben asked, hopefully.

'I do actually . . .' Santa replied.

'We were so close, Number 2! Get the helicopter. There's no way we're going to let this one go,' cried Number 1.

'Numbers 3 and 4, can you hear me?' Number 2 barked into the radio.

'Roger . . .' came the reply.

'No, this is Number 2, not Roger. He left a few months back to open a farm.'

'Oh for the love of . . .' Number 1 grabbed the radio. 'We need back-up now. We have had a close encounter with an extra-terrestrial craft and we need to pursue.' Number 1 put his hand over the radio and turned to the American family. 'By the way, if you tell anyone about this, you'll go to prison, or I might just kill you, or something worse. So, just keep quiet. Here's fifty pounds on behalf of Her Majesty's Government. Go and buy some hot dogs or something. But remember about the prison and death thing. Have a nice Christmas, guys!' Number 1 smiled and patted them on the back.

'Err . . . let's go home,' one of the tourists said, as they all dispersed.

'Taxi!' he yelled, running for the park entrance.

'And do visit again!' Number 1 yelled cheerfully after them, before turning to Number 2. 'Have you still got a reading for the UFO?'

Number 2 looked at his tracking device. 'Yes, but it doesn't make sense . . .'

'Why?'

'Well, according to this, they're on the M1, stopped at the Watford Gap services.

'Buy a map?' Ben said. 'That's your big plan?'

'When you're lost, buying a map is the obvious thing to do,' Santa said, as they got out of the sleigh.

'Right, firstly, I wasn't lost, I'd just misplaced my bearings. There's a difference. Secondly, I thought you were just going to use some pixie magic, or ask one of the reindeer or something,' Ben replied grumpily.

'We could just ask for directions?' Santa suggested.

'I don't need to ask,' Ben said. 'We just keep to the M1 until we hit Iceland.'

Santa looked at Ben. Ben looked back at Santa. 'What?' Ben asked innocently.

'Let's get a map. Do you have any money?' Santa asked, as they walked in through the automatic doors.

'Ahh, I did find some money in your sleigh, but I spent it all on carrot sticks,' Ben said, looking a bit embarrassed.

'Don't worry, I've got an idea.' Santa whispered something in Ben's ear. Ben's eyes widened with shock.

'We are not stealing a map!' Ben was horrified.

'Shh, don't tell everyone,' Santa said, trying to beckon Ben to be quiet.

'I don't care! You're Santa, you can't go around stealing stuff.'

'We don't know for sure I'm Santa,' clarified Santa.

'Oh what, the whole magic-flying-sleigh thing still hasn't convinced you?' Ben looked surprised.

'I'm yet to make a decision one way or another,' Santa said.

Ben and Father Christmas made their way into the shop. It was pretty busy still, considering how late it was—full of people making last-minute trips home to see their family, Ben supposed. He looked around—there was a couple buying some last-minute chocolates to take to a party, a husband who was desperately trying to buy something for his wife, from a late-night service station, which was nice enough that she wouldn't leave him . . . For a moment Ben felt a shiver of sadness, as he thought about his own mum and dad. He wasn't used to being so far from home. It felt especially worse, being Christmas. It was bad enough not having Dad around; now he didn't have his mum either. Ben looked a round, trying to find the maps, when he suddenly had an idea.

'Come with me,' Ben said to Santa, pulling him out of the shop.

'But the maps are this way,' Santa said, pointing at a huge shelf of books.

Soon they were standing in the walkway between the fruit machines and toilets. Ben whispered something into Santa's ear, and then he sidled off towards the cleaner.

'That's a nice bit of floor washing you've done there!' Ben said cheerfully to the cleaner.

'Err, thanks,' the cleaner said, surprised.

'What would you use for something like that?' Ben asked, acting interested.

'A mop?' the cleaner replied, completely flummoxed by his new-found admirer.

Ben mouthed 'now' to Santa, who crept in from the side, and, quiet as a mouse, pinched his bucket.

'Mop, you say . . . well, who'd have thought it.' Ben smiled.

'Yeah, well I use a mixture of detergent and soap, if you're really interested. It's a little more expensive, but worth it I feel,' the cleaner said, delighted that someone was finally noticing all his good work.

'Yeah, that's really interesting. Goodbye,' Ben said, smiling and walking away towards the automatic doors. Santa soon joined him with the newly-stolen bucket.

'What's the plan? Hit the shopkeeper with the bucket and steal a map?' Santa whispered.

'No!' Ben said. 'What's the matter with you?! You're Santa, not Genghis Khan. No, this is the plan . . .'

'Any spare change for the reindeers at Christmas?' Santa called, jangling the bucket. He looked so convincing that soon people were digging deep and handing over change by the handful. Five minutes later, Ben and Santa were leaving the service station, a map in hand, along with various pies, pasties, and chocolates to help them on their journey.

'Nice work!' Santa said, holding out his hand. 'I mean, I did say it was to help re-home reindeers, and we *are* taking them home, so it's not really fraud, is it?'

'To the North Pole!' Ben said, high-fiving Santa.

# 11

# 2000 MILES

'Hiyyyyaaaahh!' Ben yelled, pulling the reins sharply. The sleigh zoomed off into the sky, and weaved through the fluffy clouds, the taste of snow heavy in the air. There was just enough moonlight to light the way. The sleigh levelled off at several hundred feet—too high for cars and trucks to see, but too low for aeroplanes to crash into. Santa leant forward and pressed one of the buttons.

'What did you do that for?' Ben asked.

'What?'

'Why did you press that red button?'

'Oh, I don't know. Shall I turn it off?'

'No, don't turn it off. My seat is getting warmer and I can feel heat coming out by my feet. This is good, don't you see?' Ben smiled.

'Why?' Santa looked perplexed.

'It means you're remembering. You remembered about the heater; somewhere deep down, you knew what to do. We just need to let it come to the surface. Taking you back to the North Pole should help.'

'What if I don't remember?' Santa asked sadly. 'What if this is as good as it gets? Pushing the odd button and asking policemen to sit on my knee.'

'I'm sure we'll figure it out. I'll fix it,' Ben said, smiling. 'It's the least I can do.'

'Why were you taking a photograph anyway?' Santa asked.

'You're going to think it's silly . . .' Ben said, looking a bit embarrassed.

'Go on,' Santa replied.

'I wasn't sure you existed.' Ben shifted in his seat.

'Ho ho ho ho!' Santa chuckled. 'That's funny.'

'Why?' Ben turned to look at Santa.

'You weren't sure I was real, and now you're trying to persuade me that I am real!' Santa giggled.

'I suppose that is funny.' Ben started to laugh too. 'It's been quite a few hours, hasn't it . . . and by the looks of things, it's not over yet.'

Ben looked in the wing mirror. 'We've got company.'

Santa turned round and there, in the distance, were the flashing lights and whizzing rotor blades of a helicopter.

'Do you think it's those army people?' Santa said.

'Yes. I think it is. Have a look around and see if you can find a telescope, or binoculars or something.' Ben looked anxiously into the mirror.

'This can't be about trying to climb into the palace, can it?' Santa said, reaching under his seat.

'Aha, I've found one!' Santa said, pulling out a telescope. 'I really keep this sleigh well stocked, it seems.'

'I have no idea what this is about, but I don't like it.' Ben grabbed the telescope and handed the reins to Santa. 'Hold this for a second.'

'Agggh! What are you doing? I don't know how to fly this thing,' Santa said, panicking.

'You'll pick it up! Just point it straight ahead and say encouraging things to the reindeer. I'm going back here to see what I can do.' Ben climbed over the front seat towards the back where the huge sack of presents lay. He slid open the telescope and had a look at the helicopter. There was just enough light to make it out, dark and ominous, like an angry flying black pudding. It looked military, but not the normal army you see on TV at parades. This was the kind of helicopter you might see in a scary video game. What's more, it seemed to be gaining on them.

'Does this thing go any faster?' Ben asked.

'I don't know!' Santa yelled. 'I don't know even know how to fly it!'

'Well, I didn't either until about an hour ago. Think, are there any buttons you want to press? You know, like the heater one—that was excellent button-pressing. Do you have the urge to press any more buttons?' Ben asked hopefully.

'No!' Santa screamed.

'WELL, TRY!' Ben screamed back.

Nervously, Santa reached for a bright green button in the middle of the dashboard. Suddenly all the sleigh lights came on and started flashing in time to *Last Christmas* by Wham.

'Oh, that's excellent,' Ben yelled sarcastically.

A few miles back, in the helicopter cabin, Number 3 barked into the radio, 'Sir, I can see some lights up ahead. They're too low to be a plane and they keep lurching from side to side. No human pilot would do that.'

'Aaaargh, there's a moth up my nose!' Santa cried, pulling the reins left and then right.

'Do you mind?! I'm trying to work on a plan here,' Ben cried, clinging on for dear life.

'Plan? Oh phew, there's a plan! What is it?' Santa said, finally sneezing a moth out of his rosy-red hooter.

'Can I open a few presents?' Ben said, looking around him.

'Oh yeah,' Santa said, 'let's all have a party, shall we? You open the presents, I'll get some jelly and ice cream, and the reindeer can juggle. We'll invite that helicopter chasing us and we can have a right royal knees-up! What do you want to open some presents for?!' Santa cried, wresting the controls back.

'I have a plan, but I don't have what I need, and the presents are my only option,' Ben said, hunting through the sack. 'Will you promise not to shout at me?'

'Why would I shout at you?'

'Because I wouldn't have thought Santa would appreciate me opening other kids' presents!' Ben yelled back.

'Fine, just go for it!'

'Can we get any closer?' Number 1 barked into his radio.

'I'm catching up slowly. I don't know what they're using to power their craft, but it's pretty fast. We haven't got much time before fuel levels drop and we have to turn round, but I can keep chasing for now. Are you getting any readings back there, Number 2?' the co-pilot asked.

'Yes!' Number 2 said. 'It looks like some sort of organic power source . . . and there's something else too.' Number 2 hesitated. 'I'm sure I heard a sound.'

'Maybe they're trying to communicate with us!' Number 1 cried. 'This could be important.'

'Well, don't think me odd . . .' Number 2 muttered into his radio. The other three looked at each other and then back at Number 2. 'I thought I heard, "Last Christmas I gave you my heart"' Number 2 said, looking round at the others. 'What do you think that means?'

'I think it means they want their heart back, their soul, maybe they believe we have taken their souls?

This could be the beginning of an interstellar war,'
Number 1 said. 'We need to track this ship down and
stop it, by whatever means necessary.'

'Can you at least turn that music off? I like the song, I
just can't stand those stupid bells in the background!'
Ben yelled at Santa.

'I'll hit the button again,' Santa shouted back. But
it didn't work—now the lights were flashing twice as
fast and twice as bright.

'Oh bottoms,' Santa said. 'How you getting on
back there?'

'Okay, it just seems a bit weird opening other
people's presents,' Ben said, rummaging through
parcels. 'Nope—that's a My Little Pony, nah—this
one's a train set.'

'Aha!' Ben said, suddenly tearing the paper open.
'This is what I'm talking about!'

Ben pulled back the paper, revealing The
Zappo Ammo 3000—the biggest, baddest, foam-
pellet firing gun the world had ever known. Ben had

seen an advert on TV where the gun had taken out an elephant! Yes, it was a cartoon advert, but even so, Ben had to hope that it might help stop a helicopter.

Ben ripped open the package, clunked the double-action trigger, and loaded the thing with as much foam ammo as it could hold. He wrapped his blanket over his body and face until he had the appearance of a ninja ready for battle, and slowly raised himself to his feet, ready to take aim.

'Number 1, NUMBER 1, LOOK!' Number 3 yelled. 'There's some sort of creature in the distance! Look at its massive head; it must be an alien with a huge brain or something. It appears to be holding . . . a gun! It looks as though he's about to take aim.'

'EAT THIS, YOU DONKEY FACE!' Ben cocked the gun back and unleashed a barrage of tiny foam bullets straight at the helicopter, which bounced off the windscreen. PING, PING, PING! they pinged.

'We've been hit!' Number 3 cried.

'What?! No!' Number 1 screamed.

'Sir.' Number 2 reached out and held his hand, 'I don't know if this is the right time . . .'

'Damage report, Number 3,' Number 1 barked into his radio.

'But . . .' continued Number 2, 'I've always loved you. Not like a man loves a dog, or the way a person loves a football team . . . but, I mean, proper love.'

'No damage Number 1, we're fine,' Number 4

replied, 'but we're going to run out of fuel flying at this speed.'

'What?! But we're so close!' Number 1 shouted, slamming his fist into his hand. 'We'll have to turn back. If we can't catch up with speed alone we're going to need a trap. Let's carry on tracking them, and come up with a better plan to catch this thing once and for all . . . Sorry, were you saying something, Number 2 . . .?'

'Oh err, nothing, Number 1, nothing at all.'

'Yeeees! It worked, they're turning away—WOW this thing is good!' Ben said, admiring the gun. 'I need to put this on my list next year!'

'How are we doing?' Santa yelled, oblivious to what had been going on.

'All good, they've gone,' Ben said, jumping with joy.

'Good!' said Santa, 'Because you might want to come up here and see this.'

'What is it?' Ben said, making his way back to the front of the sleigh.

'I think it's the North Pole. I think we're here, Ben . . .'

# SILVER BELLS

**B**en rushed to the front of the sleigh. Santa had just about mastered control by now, and had started to descend. Between the mist and the snow glowed the far-away lights of a small town. The reindeer galloped faster, sensing that they were somewhere familiar, as though they were on autopilot, racing between the mountains and pulling the sleigh back to where it belonged.

'Do you recognize anything?' Ben asked hopefully.

'Yes, sort of. I feel as though I've been here in

a dream,' Santa said. His face was a mixture of excitement and bewilderment.

The sleigh was flying lower and lower to the ground. 'Whhhhhhooooooo!' Santa yelled.

'I think we might be going a bit fast,' Ben said, holding on tight.

'Nonsense! I know how to fly this thing!' Santa said, whipping the reins.

'I'm not so sure . . .' Ben said.

'If you could make sure your trays are in an upright position and your seatbelts are fastened, as we are coming into land,' Santa said, putting on his best captain's voice.

That, at least, was sound advice, Ben thought, as he strapped himself in. The ground was rapidly approaching and Ben could make out a tiny town. It looked like a model village—I mean, everything did from up here, but this really, really looked like one. Ben could make out gingerbread houses, with candy-cane windows, covered in snow that looked like the creamiest frosting imaginable. Hundreds and thousands peppered the windows;

strawberry laces acted as door frames. It was a town good enough to eat, and it was zooming into view at rather an alarming rate.

'How should I land?' Santa asked.

'What do you mean, how should you land? Land how you land!' Ben wailed.

'I mean, should I go for a traditional landing? I've never done this before . . . Well, I mean, I have but I just don't remember!' Santa beamed.

'What do you mean "traditional landing"? How many landings are there?!'

'Well, I could I could try landing with style; you know, make it look cool.'

'You're Santa, not The Stig! Get a grip, man!' Ben cried.

'All right, Mr Boring.'

'Just get us down.' Ben put his hands over his eyes.

'I was going to ask you something. What was it now? I think it was important . . .' Santa said, dropping the reins so he could scratch his head.

'Pick the reins up, you madman!' Ben whimpered.

The gingerbread houses were zooming towards the sleigh at what felt like a million miles an hour—Ben could feel his stomach fly up into what felt like his nose.

'Hooooold on!' Santa screamed like a child on a roller coaster who'd had too much fizzy pop and needed a wee.

THUD. The sleigh slammed on to the snow. Santa's head smacked against the dashboard, and he let out a howl as his arm crunched against the side of the sleigh. A huge puff of white powder hit Ben and Santa in the eyes. The sleigh snaked and skidded towards the gingerbread town, bumping and rattling all the way as the reindeer struggled to gain control.

'I've remembered what I was going to ask you!' Santa bellowed into Ben's ear.

'What?!' Ben howled back.

'I've remembered what I was going to ask you,' Santa shouted.

'What?!' Ben said.

'I SAID, I'VE REMEMB—'

'YES, I KNOW! WHAT'S THE THING THAT YOU'VE REMEMBERED TO ASK ME?!' Ben cried, his voice wobbling as the sleigh bounced over the ice towards the houses. Ben could see that they were about the size of sheds in real life—not much bigger than in a model village, but still big enough to hurt if one whacked you in the face.

'Do you know where the brakes are?' Santa cried. 'I'd quite like the brakes, they'd be really useful now.'

'Pull the blue lever!' Ben shouted.

Santa yanked a lever. 'You're listening to *Gardeners' World* . . '

'That's the radio! Not that lever, it's the one next to it,' Ben screamed.

Santa grabbed it. 'Phew, that was clo—!'

SMACK. The sleigh crashed into a snowdrift, bringing it to a halt.

For a second, there was silence. Santa and Ben were buried head-deep in snow. Ben managed to dig his way out and fall out of the sleigh. His head felt as though it had been hit with about forty snowballs. He staggered a few paces, and looked around. They'd managed to land in the centre of the gingerbread village.

'Santa, Santa where are you?' Ben turned round to see the top of Santa's hat sticking out of a pile of snow. 'Oh no, I've killed him, I've actually killed Santa. First I knock him out, almost killing him, now I've actually killed him.' Ben sat down in the snow. Things couldn't get any worse.

Suddenly the sound of singing filled the air. It was distant at first, but then became louder and louder. The doors of the gingerbread houses opened, and one by one tiny elves—no taller than a chair, with silver bells on their hats—tiptoed out of their houses and started to dance in the street.

'Santa's back, isn't that fine, he delivered the presents in record time!'

Over and over they sang. Then the elves started muttering to themselves and looking at their watches. And then they noticed the sleigh was mostly still full of presents. They gathered around Ben, poking and prodding him. What strange creature was this to invade their world?

'Ouch, eek, stop that!' Ben hopped about, yelping. Then suddenly, like a jack-in-a-box, Santa popped out from the snow.

'You're alive!' Ben cried. 'I didn't kill you! Oh thank goodness.'

'Oh no, I'm perfectly well, I always land the sleigh like that,' Santa said, shaking the snow out of his eyebrows.

'Always . . .?' Ben said, 'Wait a minute, what's your name?'

'My name is Santa! You know, Father Christmas, St Nicholas, the elf-in-chief.' He smiled. 'What a daft question! You would have thought the costume would have given it away . . . and who are you? You remind me of a dream I had. There was this boy and he hit me on the head . . .'

'Hit? Are you sure? It was more of a misunderstanding.' Ben smiled at the elves, who were starting to look rather annoyed.

'He tried to kidnap me . . .' Santa mused.

'He probably just wanted to prove you were real . . . Could have been any boy in the world, really . . . ' Ben, smiled again.

'In fact, now I come to think of it, it might not have been a dream.' Santa narrowed his eyes.

'Who knows! We all have odd dreams. I once dreamt I was on the Isle of Wight; doesn't really mean anything,' Ben said casually.

Santa looked round at the sleigh, and ran to the sack of presents, still half full. Santa looked at Ben, horrified.

'There are still loads of gifts to deliver. What have you done?!' Santa yelled at Ben.

'You'd lost your memory,' Ben cried in his defence.

'You're right, I'd forgotten that,' Santa said.

By now, Ben was surrounded by a mob of really-quite-angry elves. The skipping and dancing had stopped, and they looked furious. One rolled up his sleeves and strutted over towards Ben.

'Hey boss, do you want us to teach this wiseguy a lesson?' the elf said, in a thick New York accent.

'Oh my . . .' said Ben, 'Your voice is so deep.'

'Yeah, we could make this guy disappear, ba-da-boom, ba-da-bing,' another joined in.

These weren't elves, they were gangsters! Just like

the ones Ben had seen in the movies.

'No, don't hurt me. I'm nice!' Ben pleaded. It was a long shot, but maybe they wouldn't murder him if they knew he was nice.

'No, wait! He saved us from the helicopter people who were chasing me, or was that a dream?' Santa asked.

'No, that was real!' Ben pleaded.

'Aha! He is nice!' Santa agreed.

'Thank you . . .' Ben said, in an I-told-you-so sort of way.

'But we do have a problem. We need to get the rest of these presents delivered, and half the night's gone already.'

Santa reached into the sack to check how many presents were still in there. 'Ouch!' he suddenly yelped.

'Hey, what is it, boss?' a particularly gruff-looking elf asked.

'My arm, I must have hurt it in the crash . . . I mean, skilful landing,' Santa said, wincing.

'How many times do I have to say, boss, use the brakes more, you're not The Stig.'

'I totally said that too!' Ben yelled.

'I can't deliver the presents like this, it's hard enough with the amount of time we have left, let alone with this injury,' Santa said, rubbing his arm.

'Couldn't you put something on it to make it better?' Ben said hopefully.

'Like what?' Santa asked.

'I dunno . . . pixie dust?'

At that point, half a dozen elves pulled out tiny machine guns from under their pointy hats.

'PIXIES?! Let me finish him off right now,' the gruff one said.

'No, Jimmy Knuckles, I've told you before, we

don't have to resort to violence every time,' Santa said, waving his good arm around.

'I don't take kindly to being called a pixie,' Jimmy grimaced, before beckoning the other elves to put their weapons away.

'You're not what I was expecting,' Ben said, looking around at the rest of the elves.

'Don't tell me,' Jimmy started, 'little pointy ears, singing . . . Well, to be fair, we *do* do a fair bit of singing. But it ain't all prancing and farting rainbows. We're running a business here. A real slick outfit. If you got a problem with that, then I'll have a problem with you,' Jimmy said.

'I have no problem, no problem at all. Sorry about the whole pixie thing,'

'I can respect a man who can admit he was wrong. You're all right, kid.' Jimmy gestured at Ben to bend down, and he kissed him on both cheeks.

'Thanks.' Ben smiled.

'We need a plan,' Santa called out. 'I can finish off delivering the rest of the presents, but I'm going to need some help. I can probably fly the sleigh, but

I'm going to need someone to do the chimney work'
Santa said, looking at Ben.

'What?' Ben said turning round. 'Why are you all looking at me?'

'You're going to be my other Santa.'

'What?! I don't know anything about delivering stuff, or indeed "chimney work".' Ben looked around him for someone to back him up.

'The boss has made his decision, that's how this thing works,' Jimmy said, smiling.

'Jimmy, find Big Tony and take Ben to the training room. The rest of you, let's ready the sleigh, we leave in half an hour. Then we save Christmas!' Santa yelled.

'Training room, what training room?' Ben asked. 'And who's Big Tony?'

# MISTLETOE AND WINE

Ben was led to one of the gingerbread houses, and ducked as he went through the door. Inside it was like a little Italian restaurant with tiny round tables, each with tiny check tablecloths on. There at the back, sitting in the half-light, was a slightly older, rounder elf than the others Ben had seen.

'Wait here,' Jimmy whispered, as he wandered over to talk to the lone figure.

'Big Tony will see you now,' Jimmy yelled to Ben, waving him down. 'You show this guy some respect, or there'll be trouble, if you know what I mean.'

'Righty-ho,' Ben said nervously.

The elf had a round chubby face that he was dabbing with an oversized napkin. He was sitting in front of a big plate of spaghetti and meatballs sat in the middle of the table. Without looking up, the elf spoke.

'I hear you'se got a problem you need fixing. Something about wanting to be a Santa or some such kind. Do I hear correctly?' he asked.

'Yes, Mr Tony, Mr Big Tony . . . ' Ben said nervously. 'I was hoping you might be able to help. I would be very grateful.'

'I heard that you'se interested in training to be some sort of substitute Santie Claus, doos I hear this correctly too?' Tony asked, taking a sip from a glass of frothy milk.

'Yes please. I think that's the plan, I'd really owe you one.' Ben smiled.

'Aha, a favour for a favour. I likes how you think.' Big Tony smiled, at last looking up. 'Would you like a cigar?'

'Not for me, I'm too little,' Ben said graciously.

'NOT THAT THERE'S ANYTHING WRONG WITH BEING LITTLE! I like little people, I mean, I like all people, especially elves.'

'I prefer diminutive; we elves are diminutive people.'

'Yes, those, I like all of those, EXCEPT PIXIES!' Ben added quickly.

'This kid is very wise,' Big Tony said. 'And the cigar is just chocolate.'

Big Tony took a bite and leaned back in his chair.

'You're not a fan of pixies I see—so you're a quick learner too.' Big Tony nodded, untucking the napkin from his collar. 'Now let's go to work.'

Big Tony got up and walked to the back of the restaurant, through the kitchens and into another room. It was Santa's workshop, only it wasn't filled with elves whittling trains with tiny hammers and tools, it was filled giant machines and mechanical robots, smashing down, cutting, moulding, and lasering toys of every size and shape. Ben couldn't believe his eyes.

'Not what you were expecting, kid, am I right?' Big Tony asked.

'No.'

Ben watched as everywhere they went, elves would kiss the hand of Big Tony. It seemed as though he was feared and loved in equal measure.

'We used to use magic dust and sing-songs to make the toys, but we're competing with China and Apple these days, so we've modernized the whole outfit.'

'This way,' Big Tony said, holding open the door to another room. 'This is the training room.'

'Wow!' Ben said. There was a replica of a house, complete with chimney, fireplaces, and kids' bedrooms.

'Angel!' Big Tony yelled. 'Come here, I need something.' Suddenly a lady elf, an elfette—Ben wasn't quite sure of the right word—appeared from a side door. She had bright-red lipstick and a tape measure round her neck.

'What is it, honey pie?' she asked. 'Aggh!' she screamed, looking at Ben who, couldn't help but tower over all the elves.

'I need you to fix this fella up with a suit,' Big Tony said. 'Something real classy!'

'Yeah, we got no time at all,' Jimmy chipped in.

'OK, anything for you, Big Tony.' Angel smiled, and began to take Ben's measurements.

'Can't I just deliver presents in what I'm wearing?' Ben asked.

Everyone laughed. 'No, we need to give the illusion that you are Santa, in case any kids wake up. It's important they think they've seen the big fella, or the firm's reputation is ruined,' Big Tony said.

'Plus, how do you think you're going to get down the chimney?' Jimmy asked.

'I could climb?' Ben asked, and once again everyone laughed.

'You've met Santa, right? Well he is a little too fond of the *penne con zucchini* to be slim enough to be going down chimneys. He needs a little help, that's why we use the suit. The red suit is not just a fashion item, as terrific as it looks; it also has the properties of allowing its owner to become very thin and fit down any chimney,' Big Tony explained.

'How? Is it magic?' Ben asked.

Once again everyone laughed. 'No, dearie!' Angel said. 'Ain't you a sweetie. It's a mixture of polycarbon fibres—technology that allows the recipient to slim down to the same shape as their surroundings.'

'What does that mean?' Ben said, totally confused.

'It means it's a magic suit.' She winked. 'I'll have this ready in ten minutes. That OK?'

'Beautiful, sweet cheeks,' Big Tony said, grinning. 'Let's get on with the training! Imagine you're down the chimney and in the living room. What do you do next?'

'I look around and make sure there are no things to trip over, like trip-wires or something . . .'

'What kind of a maniac leaves trip-wires out for Santa?' Jimmy Knuckles asked.

'I can't imagine . . . Anyway, I look around and put the presents under the tree.'

'Yes, because it's that simple,' Jimmy said, shaking his head. 'I'm sorry, Big Tony, I've wasted your time. This kid ain't got it. I'm going to have to whack him.'

'WHAT!' Ben cried. 'You're going to kill me?!'

'No! Whack you with some knowledge,' Jimmy replied.

'There are a million things to think about when you're delivering presents,' Big Tony interrupted. 'Firstly, you got to get into the place. What happens if the chimney is blocked? We're talking using drainpipes and open windows. Now, the suit will allow you to do this, but you'se have to tell it where to go. Then once you're inside, you have to look out for dogs and cats. If there are floorboards, you might have to take your boots off, then there are the dangers of roller skates, toy cars, lego bricks all lying around.'

All the elves in the room winced at the thought of stepping on a lego brick.

'All these things can make you fall, and also make lots of noise, which all leads to detection. Some kids like their presents by the tree, others at the bottom of their bed, and you can bet that for every ten children, five will be trying to stay awake for Santa. Then there's the admin side of it. Milk and cookies have been left out, you gotta have a sip and bite, some people leave carrots out for Rudolph, not the other reindeer—Dasher, Dancer, Prancer, Vixen, Comet, Cupid, Donner, and Blitzen.'

'Oh, that's what they're called!' Ben said under his breath.

Big Tony continued: 'Now it's not Rudolph's fault, but the other reindeer get jealous. Did you know that reindeer are a very jealous species?'

'No,' Ben said.

'Well they are, so you have to manage their feelings too. Make sure they don't feel left out. Then, some kids want a signed letter from Santa. Now you can't give Johnny a signed letter, but not one to Stacey down the road. What Johnny gets, Stacey gets too. Then there's present distribution. Bigger presents at the back, or most valuable at the back—which is it? You've got to make a split-second decision. The name of the game is 'get in and get out'. You have to remain undetected at all times. What happens if you wake someone up? Do you hide or charge out of the house? Sometimes police can be called. Now, we have a little arrangement with the cops—and they understand that we need time to get the job done—but what happens if a cop isn't in the know? What if he's not interested in making some kiddie happy for Christmas, he just wants to arrest someone? What then? Show me. There's a house right here, what are you going to do? Show me how you're going to deliver presents. Don't think of yourself as Santa, but more as a gift-giving ninja. Can you do that? Can you? Do you have what it takes, kid? Can you be the best sneaker in the world? Huh, kid?!'

'YEEEEEES!' Ben roared. Big Tony's speech had been relentless, like a machine gun of words being fired at him. And Ben was pumped up.

'Yes, I am King of Sneaking. I am your man!' Ben yelled.

'Good, so prove it,' Big Tony said, smiling.

Ben walked over to the living room. There was a sack of presents there by the chimney.

'Ready?' Big Tony asked.

'Ready,' Ben said.

'Let's do training level 3,' Big Tony said, pushing a big button on the wall, and slipping on some night-vision goggles.

All the lights went out, and the place was plunged into darkness. Ben picked up the sack and tiptoed towards the tree. Suddenly he stopped. One of the floorboards began to creak. Ben tiptoed back the other way. Again, the floorboards creaked. Then suddenly, from behind the sofa, a mechanical dog appeared. Instinctively, Ben rolled across the room, landing by the dog. He stroked it on the head and the dog's eyes closed. Ben had stopped the dog barking but now he was even further away from the tree, with a creaky floorboard in his way. Ben wiped the beads of sweat from his forehead and looked up. There was a string of Christmas decorations running across the ceiling. Ben jumped on the sofa and, like an army recruit, grabbed the decorations and started swinging along them towards the tree. About halfway across, Ben felt the string start to give way. Thinking quickly, he let go and leaped across to grab the curtain. Ben used it like a rope, swinging

it backwards and
forwards to propel
himself along. As soon
as he had enough
momentum, Ben ran across
the wall, over the floorboards,
and landed into a roly-poly,
coming to a stop by the
Christmas tree, the
presents spilling out
of the sack perfectly
underneath. They couldn't
have been better placed if Ben had
used his hands. With that, Ben walked
towards the door, nibbled the biscuit, and
downed a shot of milk before walking as cool as
you like, out of the training house.

'This kid's got skills,' Big Tony said, chomping
on his chocolate cigar. 'Let's do this.'

# LITTLE SAINT NICK

A few moments later Ben was standing in the snow in his red suit, looking like a mini Santa.

'You've done a cracking job, Angel,' Ben smiled.

'Ain't you a sweetie,' Angel giggled.

Ben giggled too, before catching Big Tony's eye, who was looking less pleased.

'Ahem, how does the suit make me go all thin and chimney-shaped?' Ben asked, pressing one of the buttons down the middle. 'What does this do?'

'That keeps the cold out, sweetie. It's this button.'

'Oh,' Ben said.

'All you gotta do is jump down the chimney, the suit will do the rest,' Big Tony interrupted.

'Aha, there you are, my lad,' Santa said, emerging from the back of the sleigh, his arm in a sling. 'How was training?'

'Good!' Ben said.

'And the suit; did Angel work wonders for you?'

Ben caught sight of Big Tony again. 'Yes, it was all fine, thank you. How's the arm?'

'Hurts like I don't know what, but what can you do. The reindeer are fed and watered, I've had a Scotch egg and a wee, so I think we're all ready to go.'

'Well, what can I say, Big Tony, it's been lovely. Thanks for everything,' Ben said hurriedly.

'Knuckles and Big Tony, we'll still need your help with any problems we may encounter along the way, so hop aboard. There's not a lot of room, so we might all have to squish up, maybe even sit on each other's laps. I hope that's okay,' Santa said, climbing into the sleigh and getting the reindeer ready for take-off.

'Goodbye, sweetie!' Angel said to Ben, before

jumping up and giving him a kiss.

'Oh no, I'm a dead man,' Ben muttered, looking anxiously over at Big Tony.

'Right, the fact of the matter is we are hopelessly behind. If we don't get all these presents delivered, we may find that the world collapses and humankind is destroyed for good. I know that sounds a bit over-dramatic, but think about it. Once the Christmas spirit is gone, it just doesn't come back. It doesn't take a year off then return next year. It's gone for good. Think of all the trouble that will make, think of kids waking up and thinking that no one loves them, or that the world is uncaring and doesn't want them to be happy. They will grow up angry and hurt. Angry and hurt people do bad things. There could be riots down there. They might take it out on their parents or each other, and one-by-one, like ripples on a pond the whole thing escalates, and the world might never recover. I'm talking wars. The breakdown of basic government. I'm talking people having to eat their own cats to stay alive. Selling elderly relatives to buy wood, to keep their rudimentary shelters warm. The end of the world as we know it. So try to have a good one, chaps!' Santa smiled.

Ben, Big Tony, and Jimmy Knuckles all looked at each other and gulped.

Meanwhile, at a secret military base in the north of England, a helicopter was being prepared for its next mission. Engines were being checked, extra fuel was being added and, more worryingly, missiles and guns were being attached, checked, and double-checked.

'OK guys,' Number 1 said, taking off his helmet. 'Numbers 2, 3, and 4, sit down.'

They all sat on upturned crates beneath the dormant helicopter. Each of them had identical moustaches—it was part of the uniform—the theory being that if they all looked the same it would confuse the enemy, but it also confused anyone who wasn't the enemy too.

'Team meeting. I want us to do some blue-sky thinking. You know, fly up a few ideas and see who

whistles. Let's think outside the box.' Number 1
stood up and started to walk around the hangar.
'We here at X Squadron, need to get some results. I
didn't want to have to tell you this, but unless we get
proof of aliens soon, the squadron's being disbanded.
No more hunting round looking for aliens; we might
actually have to go somewhere dangerous. It'll be
like that team-building exercise at Laser Quest we
had the other month.'

'Ooh, that was fun!' Number 3 smiled.

'Yes, except they won't be using lasers, they'll be using bullets, and we won't get fries and a bottle of pop afterwards, we'll probably get taken to hospital, and instead of it being indoors, round the back of Asda, it'll be in a muddy field. In fact, the more I think about it, Laser Quest is a terrible comparison. In other words, it'll be terrible.'

'Sir?'

'Yes, Number 4.'

'Actually, it's Number 2.'

'Oops, sorry, it's the moustache, you know.'

'Why UFOs? I mean, I think we all have different reasons for taking this assignment. For me it was *Star Trek*, and I know Number 4 wants to find Elvis, and Number 3 says he's been abducted by aliens several hundred times; what about you, sir?'

Number 1 looked off into the distance, drifting into an old childhood memory. He was remembering himself as a little boy—always watching sci-fi shows on TV. All he wanted that Christmas was his own UFO toy. He wrote to Father Christmas, but with each present he unwrapped on Christmas morning, the more disappointed he became. There was no UFO—just a pair of dancing shoes and some chocolate coins. For years he was forced to go to tap-dancing lessons, but Number 1 had no rhythm, and he became a joke on the tap-dancing circuit. Oh how the others teased him. From that day forth, he vowed that if he ever wanted to see a UFO himself, he would have to do it on his own. No more letters to Father Christmas.

Number 1 wiped a tear from his eye. 'I just want to find out the truth, that's all.'

Suddenly, the tracking system bleeped into life. Number 1 grabbed it. 'They've just entered American airspace. We end this tonight,' Number 1 said, eyeing up the missiles on the helicopter.

# FAIRYTALE OF NEW YORK

'Where are we?' Ben cried, looking below him.

'We're flying over Canada, headed for New York,' Santa smiled. 'Look, you can see the Statue of Liberty waving at us.'

Ben turned round to see Jimmy Knuckles and Big Tony fast asleep, curled up next to each other.

'They're a sleepy bunch, elves. They work so hard they need regular naps,' Santa said, turning round to see what Ben was looking at.

'They're not what I was expecting,' Ben said.

'More gangstery?' Santa asked. 'It can be a shock

when you first meet them. Not many people expect elves to be so cross about so many things.'

'Yes, and I wasn't expecting the guns either,' Ben said.

'They're just spud guns, but don't tell them I said so. They like to think they're tough, but mostly it's all talk, except when it comes to pixies. They really don't like those guys.'

'Why?' Ben asked.

'It goes back to the fairy wars of a few decades ago. Before then, elves, pixies, trolls, and fairies all used to live in the woods. They helped the flowers to grow, tidied the trees, polished the rainbows, and all that, and they were all friends. Soon enough though, cities got bigger, and forests got smaller. It was only a matter of time before the two worlds collided. Polishing rainbows is rather boring, compared to the bright lights of a big city. The fairies moved into the city, doing good deeds, collecting teeth, that sort of thing. The elves, well, they liked to make things— toys and such, and fixing cars on the side. Pixies, on the other hand, liked to take things. They worked with the elves at first, helping get all the things they needed, alongside the trolls. But then the pixies got greedy and decided to steal from the elves. It was easy, as they were so sleepy, and the trolls, being idiots, got talked into working for the pixies. There was a huge fight and the pixies, with the help of the trolls, fought the elves. The fairies tried to stop it all but it got very messy. That's why the elves fled somewhere safe to hide. They ended up at the North Pole. Christmas is the only time the elves are let back into the cities again, sort of like a peace agreement.'

'Crikey,' Ben said, shaking his head, 'I had no idea . . . I'll be careful about what I say, next time I mention a pixie or a troll.'

Ben looked over the edge of the sleigh. 'I always wanted to see New York from the sky.' Ben grinned looking down at the city below. 'Can I ask you a question . . .?'

'It's magic . . .'

'What is?'

'The sleigh,' Santa replied. 'You were going to ask me how I manage to get all the presents delivered in one night, right? That's the one question I always get asked. Well, the sleigh has a magic aura around it, like a force field, which means I can work super-fast and visit all the kids in the world. It sort of slows time around it. For every hour in the sleigh it's about ten seconds in the real world. It means I can spend five hours flying around a big city like London and only fifty seconds has gone by in real-world time.'

'Oh . . .' Ben nodded. 'A bit like dog years. I did wonder . . . How long have you been doing this job, I mean have you always been Santa?'

'Oh no, I've had lots of jobs. My dad was Santa, and his dad before him. I think I just fancied a change. I used to be a court jester—that Elizabeth I, cor, she had a sense of humour on her. She liked the physical comedy, custard pies and things like that, but also the observational stuff too. Then I worked as a gravedigger during the black death—goodness, that was a busy winter. I was a baker during the Great Fire of London—that was a bad gig. I got fired on my first day. Then I was a milkman for a while, and then I worked in a post office. I was left-back for Arsenal for a bit too—we won the double—before I went on to try my hand at acting. Have you ever seen *Star Wars*?'

'Err, yeah . . .' Ben nodded.

'I was the third Stormtrooper from the back. I was part of an urban hip-hop collective during the Britpop years—we even toured with Oasis. Great days. Anyway, I guess being Santa was my true calling. It's in your blood. So when Dad retired, I stepped into his boots, quite literally.'

'How old are you?' Ben was barely able to contain his astonishment.

'Nearly seven-hundred, I think. To be honest, after forty I stopped counting. There's only so many big birthdays one can celebrate. Right, buckle up, time to get delivering. We're going to do the city block-by-block. Here's the list—all you have to do is get in and get out. Once you've done your first, it'll be easy. I'll send in Big Tony to help you, and I'll take Jimmy Knuckles and do what I can. OI, YOU TWO, NAP TIME'S OVER. TIME TO WORK!' Santa yelled to the two sleepy elves. The sleigh swooped down and with pinpoint precision, landed on top of an apartment block. Ben had never been to America before, but it felt like how it was always meant to feel, even the sound of distant police cars was perfect. Ben hopped out, along with Big Tony, who was holding all the presents. Santa was right, something felt different, like the world had stopped turning, like everything had slowed down. Big Tony nodded towards the vent in the corner.

'That's the closest to a chimney we're gonna get. I'll meet you down there,' he said, and with that, hurled himself down.

Ben listened as the metal echoed with the sounds of Big Tony thumping and clanging down the vent. It sounded very twisty-turny, like going down a water slide, only more painful. Ben put one foot in, and something odd began to happen. It was as if his foot was made of plasticine and it was being stretched so it got longer and thinner. It felt like it did when pins and needles start to go; tickly, but also weird and confusing. Ben put his other leg in and put his hand on top of the vent, and, swinging himself down, let go. Suddenly his whole body felt long and thin like a snake. Ben wailed, then remembered that wailing was probably a bad idea—he bit his fist so he wouldn't make any noise. The vent seemed to go on for miles. Ben felt like he'd been falling for hours, as he slithered between floors, occasionally getting a glimpse of various apartments through the tiny gaps in the air vent. Eventually, Ben landed in the middle of an apartment like a puddle of rainwater. He stood up and checked his body parts to see if they were all still working correctly. That's when he noticed Big Tony. He was motionless in front of Ben. There, between them and the Christmas tree, was a dog. A big one, a big growling one; a big growling, snarling, angry one.

'Why can't we just walk round him? If the world slows down, we can just outrun him,' Ben whispered.

'It works with humans, but dogs operate in a different time zone; they see us as we see them. That's why sometimes you see a dog barking at nothing—there's probably been some sort of magic creature around,' Big Tony muttered out of the corner of his mouth.

'What do we do?' Ben asked, petrified.

'We take him out,' Tony said.

'What? Kill him?!' Ben bellowed.

'Shhh, no, we don't kill him. We let him out while we get our work done. Find something small to throw. Something he could nibble on.'

Ben looked round but there was nothing; the apartment was plush and modern, and everything was sleek, with clean lines. Suddenly Ben had an idea.

'Have you found anything yet?' Big Tony whispered. He turned round to see Ben measuring him with his hands. 'You're not going to throw me!' Big Tony snapped.

'Oh come on, look at him, he thinks you're a small . . . I mean *diminutive* chew toy.'

'You can't go around throwing elves,' Big Tony cried.

'Why?' Ben asked.

'Well . . . I . . . I don't know, it feels wrong.' Big Tony turned with his hands on his hips.

'Look, it's just this once. Next place we're in, I'll get a load of cookies and we can use them as doggy

146

treats. I don't want to come across all corporate here, but we are on the clock, you know, and we don't have a lot of time,' Ben said, looking at his watch. 'Please?'

'Fine. But if this gets out, that I'm some kind of chew toy, some kind of clown to amuse dogs, only here to make them happy, you're gonna pay.'

'Deal.' Ben grabbed Big Tony by the belt and collar, and with one motion, threw him into the corner of the room. Big Tony landed on the polished floor and skidded into the wall. The dog started wagging his tail immediately, and went to play fetch, licking and nuzzling Big Tony like he was a dolly. Ben used the opportunity to grab the sack and place the presents neatly under the tree.

'All done, T! Come on, we can go now,' Ben smiled, 'First one done and no problems at all!'

Big Tony picked up the sack and, wiping the dog slime off his face, walked towards the door. 'Yep, no problems at all,' he grumbled, straightening his tiny hat. 'Only several million more to go. It's going to be a long night, kid.'

# JOY TO THE WORLD

Over the next few hours Ben, Santa, Big Tony, and Jimmy Knuckles darted all over America: from the big cities to the smallest towns, through the grandest fireplaces to the tiniest slivers in the windows, from the smallest gifts, to brand new bikes. Ben and Santa delivered them all, hopping from country to country, continent to continent, chasing the darkness across the world as they went.

'Come on Tony, keep up!' Ben called out as Big Tony carefully inspected a chimney entrance.

'Just hang on. You've been doing this job a

couple of hours, and you're telling me what to do? I'm a pro, kid, and some of these kids are pros too—they take coffee to bed so they can stay awake. Some of them sleep by the door and at the bottom of the chimney, so that Santa will have to sneak past them. Now hopefully, parents will be doing their part too. I mean, making sure that they're tired out and in bed at a reasonable time, but they have a lot on too. They've got Auntie Mabel coming round with Uncle Bertie for a big slap-up dinner—Mabel tells embarrassing stories, and Bertie has wind—the point is, they have a lot on. Add an excited and mischievous kid to the mix, and it's a recipe for disaster. Kids are out to get you. Then there's the reading the list and checking it twice problem. One slip-up, you read the wrong address, and soon enough the world's got the presents for next door, and they've got yours. So don't be telling me how to do my job.'

'Sorry, I was just saying—' Ben started.

'Well, don't! This chimney looks good, so get going,' Big Tony said, giving Ben a push.

Ben closed his eyes and held his nose, like he

was at a school swimming lesson. He opened them to find himself tumbling out of a fireplace. Ben gasped in horror. Big Tony landed seconds later.

'Oh no . . .' Tony sighed. 'We've got a Code Red.'

Ben gazed around the dark living room. It was like being in a spider's web; there were threads and ropes in every direction.

'Some kid has set a trap. There are ropes everywhere, trying to cause the big guy to trip and make a noise. It's usually some brat who wants proof that he's real, a photo for his mates at school. You know the sort. Horrible, spoilt, risks the whole of Christmas for everyone, just so they can get their glimpse. What makes them so special, is what I want to know,' Big Tony snarled, looking at Ben.

'I just wanted to say hi,' Ben protested.

'Oh, I might have known you were one of those kids. Do you know the jeopardy you put Christmas in?'

'Sorry! I did also say sorry to Father Christmas!'

'Well, sorry isn't going to help us now. How are we going to get round this lot?'

'Wait a second, I know how to beat this. I *am* this kid, I mean, I invented the Code Red. I'm the one who actually trapped Santa. I can get us out of this,' Ben said excitedly. 'Now, keep your voice down, the kid will probably be nearby, waiting.'

'And there was me about to sing a rousing chorus of *I've Got a Lovely Bunch of Coconuts*, but

'I guess now I'll just whisper instead,' Big Tony said, shaking his head.

'Do you want my help or not?' Ben sighed.

'Yes, well I suppose so,' Big Tony said, looking shifty.

'OK, OK,' Ben said, looking around, 'I see what they've done. It's a basic spiral trap. The ropes go out in an anti-clockwise direction—they are probably attached to triggers, like bells or other warning devices. Judging by the direction they're going, the child is asleep behind the sofa. That would be where I'd hide. So the only way to deal with this is to go through the centre of the room. It's the most complicated route to get to the tree, but it's the quickest. Pass me the sack.' Ben's eyes fixed on the layout of the room, and he held out his hand. Big Tony handed him the presents.

'Are you sure you're up to this level of sneakiness?' Big Tony asked.

'This is what I do,' Ben said, grabbing the presents from Big Tony. He rolled across the floor, jumping and weaving between the trip-wires and ropes, before coming to a skidding halt by the tree. Ben scattered the presents down and looked behind the sofa—sure enough, there was a boy, fast asleep. He looked about the same age as Ben. He smiled to himself and before the boy even had time to open his eyes, Ben was gone.

Ben and Big Tony spent the rest of the night working their socks off. House after house, some friendly, others not so much. They even started to get a system going. Big Tony would go first, check out the lay of the land, see if there were any dangers, and hoot like an owl if things were all clear. Then Ben would slide down, put the presents out, and then they'd both have a bite or a slurp of something and head on to the next place. The faster they went, the more time slowed down and the more progress they'd make. They were even as quick, if not quicker than Santa—although I'm not sure being quicker than a one-armed seven-hundred year-old man is much of a boast. Between all four of them, they'd done almost half the world. Ben had no idea there were so many houses, let alone so many presents.

Some kids wanted expensive video-game consoles, while others wanted the strangest things, like a top hat or a train whistle. Some people left out milk, while others left out exotic sweets and tropical punch. They came across all sorts of pets, from cats and dogs, to parrots and monkeys in hotter parts of the world. Wherever they went, though, Ben did notice one thing—all animals loved to play with elves. Ben thought it was something to do with the fact they had bells on their hats and looked a little bit like walking, talking toys. By the time they'd gone over the Pacific Ocean, Big Tony had been licked, nibbled, chased, and hugged by every species known to man.

'This is amazing!' Ben cried, as they headed back to the sleigh after another successful present drop. 'I think I'm finally getting the hang of it, I've only woken up 3,495 children, 7,594 cats and alarmed two old ladies from Arkansas. How are we doing for time?'

'We're still an hour or so behind, but it could be a lot worse,' Jimmy Knuckles yelled. 'It all depends on how Europe goes.'

'Well, that should be a doddle. I mean, it should be as easy as America,' Ben smiled. Everyone looked at him. 'What?'

'We still have to do the Prince of Transilmania.' Santa sighed.

'Who's that?' Ben asked.

The Prince of Transilmania is no ordinary child. He is the only child of the King and Queen of Transilmania, a tiny but interesting country in the heart of Europe. It's famous for two things—having a mountain and being the smallest country in Europe. Crown Prince Hector is one of the most spoilt and protected children in the world. Now, don't get me wrong, the boy is perfectly pleasant—it's the parents that are the problem. They worry. They worry a lot. And nothing is too much for their precious son. They took him swimming in the lake that lies beneath the mountain once. A risky enough trip when you're a worrying Mum and Dad who just happen to be a King and Queen. Poor Hector found the water a little chilly, because, well, because it's a lake. So being the kind parents that they are, they got it heated at great expense. Imagine that! Filling a lake full of hot water. Also, because they are very rich, and worry that someone will steal their precious little baby, they have him protected twenty-four hours a day. And when I say protected, I mean it. He has soldiers stood outside the door, ready to guard against kidnap, and even to take Hector for a wee in the middle of the night, just in case he stubs his toe. Not only does this make it very hard for Hector to get out, it makes it almost impossible for Santa to get in.

'Well, can't we just leave him? I mean, if he has everything that he wants, a soldier to take him to the loo, and a hot lake, what can he possibly want for Christmas?' Ben asked.

'Oh, man.' Jimmy Knuckles shook his head.

'Do you want me to teach this guy a lesson?' Big Tony said, pulling out his spud gun.

'No, no!' Santa said. 'Christmas isn't just about presents, it's about giving someone something they need. I get letters from all over the world, and try to answer all of them eventually. I get to see people's innermost thoughts, not the things they ask their parents and family for, but what they really need. It's like looking into someone's head and seeing their wishes. You see, Hector doesn't really need a warm lake, or hats made of emeralds. What he really needs is this . . .' Santa said, passing a letter to Ben. It was written in thick red crayon.

Dear Santa, could you please give me back my bear? I lost him a long time ago and I miss him. I can't sleep without him. I'm worried he misses me too. Lots of love, Hector.

'Part of the reason there are so many guards around Hector's bedroom is because he walks around a lot. He's not trying to escape, he's just looking for his bear,' Santa smiled. 'That's my job. I've been searching for his bear for nearly a year now, and I found it, flying over London earlier this evening. He must have left it there last time he came for a visit.'

Ben slumped into his seat. He felt a wall of sadness hit him. He felt heavy and small.

'Big Tony, and Jimmy—can you go and prepare for Hector's present drop? What's the matter, Ben?' Santa asked.

'Nothing,' Ben shrugged.

'You're not fooling me—something's the matter.'

'Did you read my letter?' Ben asked. 'I don't want to sound like it's all about me—I know it's not. I know there are children who have virtually nothing compared to me. But, I only wanted one thing. Did you see my letter?'

'I saw it, Ben. You want Christmas with your Dad, right?' Santa said, looking off into the distance.

'Yes.'

'Sometimes, Ben, there's only so much I can do. With the bear, it was easy—I have fairies, trolls and even pixies,' Santa whispered, 'to be my ears and eyes on the ground.'

'It's fine, I shouldn't have asked,' Ben said, feeling embarrassed.

'I can make most people's Christmas wishes come true, and maybe I'll make yours come true one day too. But not everything is always straightforward.

Maybe your Dad's very busy. That doesn't mean he doesn't care for you, it just means that these things are a little more complicated.'

Ben felt his cheeks burn with shame. He felt embarrassed for asking in the first place—stupid for thinking that Santa could help. Yet at the same time, he felt it was unfair—why should Hector, the boy who has everything, get his stupid bear back when he could easily buy another one, or maybe even a million more bears.

'Let's talk about this later—things will work out in the end,' Santa said, clutching Ben's hand. 'It'll be OK . . .'

'Darn it!' Number 1 yelled, 'we keep losing them!'

'They keep flying under the radar, and it's hard to keep track of them,' Number 3 cried. 'They seem to be

weaving around every house in the world, and then they speed away. It's as though they're deliberately trying to lose us.'

'They know we're after them. They are clearly a very advanced species, maybe even psychic. They seem to know our every move,' Number 1 said, scratching his helmet in confusion.

'Wait, wait!' Number 4 cried, pulling out a map. 'I've been charting their progress. See how they appear here, then here again? There's a pattern—they're circumnavigating the globe. Why are we bothering to chase them, when we could lie in wait for them? According to my predictions, they should be landing in Transilmania in a few minutes.'

'Brilliant! Let's head them off and . . .' SMACK! Number 1 slapped his fist into his hands.

# DING DONG MERRILY ON HIGH

'We need to land this thing.' Santa pointed into the night. 'Look, there's the castle.'

The sky was an inky blue now. Dawn was still some way off, but it was starting to get a touch lighter. Ben could make out mountains in the distance and the shadowy outline of a huge castle. It looked like something from a fairytale. Ben could imagine men in shiny suits of armour battling dragons to save princesses with long, impractical hairdos. Snow sat on top of each turret, and there was a dim glow from the odd light that was left on to help light the vast castle. The bells in the tower clanged the top of the hour.

'OK,' Ben said, 'what's the plan?'

'Oh nothing too different to what we're used to, we just need to take a few extra precautions,' Santa smiled. 'Here, you take the baseball bat. Knives for you, Jimmy, and the usual machine gun for you, Big Tony.'

'Thanks, boss.' Big Tony grinned as though he was greeting an old friend.

'Baseball bats, knives, guns?!' Ben yelled.

'You'll be fine. You've used a baseball bat before, right?' said Santa.

'I haven't even used one for baseball, let alone anything else! Why are there stars stuck on it?' Ben said, looking down at the bat.

'Well, it is Christmas. Just because it could be used as a weapon, doesn't mean it can't be cheery!' Santa beamed.

'Oh yeah, I mean, I wouldn't want anyone to think I wasn't wishing them a Happy Christmas as I tried to knock their block off.' Ben shook his head.

'Now listen, kid,' Tony said, grabbing Ben by his false beard. 'No one said you had to bash anyone with it—it's just a precaution. That's why I carry this semi-automatic spud gun, and Jimmy over there carries some plastic knives.'

Ben glanced over to see Jimmy practising stabbing himself in the belly.

'The plastic blades retract into the handles with every motion—great distraction technique. And you've got a rubber baseball bat to wave around. Now, if you'se got a problem with that, you and me need to have a discussion about a few things, if you know what I mean,' Big Tony said, smiling and patting Ben on the head, which sounds way more friendly than it was.

'Problem? No, I haven't got a problem. Just making sure I know what's what. Let's get ready to cause some fake injury to total strangers!' Ben grinned.

'Now you're getting into the Christmas spirit!' Santa smiled. 'Right, so here's the plan . . .'

Moments later they were on the ground, walking towards the castle.

'I don't see why it has to be me! I mean, it is my first day being Santa. I don't see why I should be the one doing the most dangerous work!' Ben said, kicking a stone as he strolled towards the moat.

'Because you're the fittest, the youngest, and the smallest Father Christmas here,' Jimmy snapped. 'Now quit your bellyaching. All you and Big Tony have to do is sneak past the guards, scale the wall, and deliver the presents while Santa and I cause a distraction. Got it?' Jimmy Knuckles asked, in such a way that Ben felt he had no choice but to say yes.

'Yes.' Ben nodded.

'Right, there are the guards. You two go round the back, and we'll keep them busy round this end.'

Ben and Big Tony ran through the bushes and round to the back of the castle. They pushed their way through a thick bank of trees and into a clearing.

'You have to do this every year?' Ben said, catching his breath.

'Yep, it's the only way to get the job done. We did try and use drones one Christmas, but the guards shot them down. It rained Nintendo DS's round here for a week.' Big Tony huffed, stopping to size up the situation. 'We need to go in this way.' Big Tony pointed to the wall.

'What way?' Ben asked, confused. 'All I can see is a drainpipe.'

Big Tony nodded.

'Wait, we're going up the drainpipe?!'

'It's the only way. Just remember to hold on tight. It's icy up there, and we don't want another accident. I really miss Paulie.' He sighed, sadly.

'Paulie? What happened to Paulie?!' Ben felt panic rising in his chest.

'He wasn't as bouncy as you'd have thought. Let's just put it this way, falling is bad for your elf,' Big Tony replied ominously.

'You're making a pun? Someone met a sticky end, and you're making puns!' Ben snarled.

'He lived, he was fine. He just works in a different department, now. I.T., if you must know.'

Ben was relieved to hear it. 'Oh, I see, so he's not dead?'

'He's fine. He just walks with a stick these days, and his eyes are a little crossed, but deep down, beneath the screaming and the shakes, it's still Paulie in there . . . Right, you go first!' Big Tony said, suddenly giving Ben a lift up, with the sharp end of his boot.

Meanwhile, on the other side of the castle, Santa and Jimmy Knuckles were approaching the main gates.

'The old travelling circus routine?' Jimmy asked.

'Yes, it works like a charm.'

A couple of guards holding torches and guns emerged from the gates.

'Halt, who goes there?' one yelled.

'Hello!' Santa called out in a high-pitched, over-the-top manner. 'My name is Gonzo. I am but a poor clown from the travelling circus. I wonder if my tiny clown assistant and I may use your lovely house for a—how you say—wee-wee?'

'Yes, good people, we are just a couple of clowns who need a little comfort break. Won't you let two innocent old entertainers use your lovely toilets?' added Jimmy Knuckles.

'Which circus are you from, and why are you dressed like Santa Claus and his elf?' asked one of the guards, shining a light in Santa's face.

'Just an ordinary travelling circus, and yes, you're right, I am dressed like Father Christmas. It's all part of the act in which I do some juggling and then saw an elf in half.'

'Saw a what in half?' the other guard said.

'This guy.' The first guard shone his torch at Jimmy. 'I think he's supposed to be an elf.'

'Isn't that what magicians do?' the first guard added, putting his gun down. 'Clowns don't saw people in half, do they?'

'I do!' Santa said, thinking on his feet.

'I loves me a bit of magic,' the other guard

chipped in, also putting his gun down.

'More than juggling?' asked Jimmy nervously.

'Both are great. It's ages since I've been to the circus,' the other guard replied. 'I was supposed to take the kids ages ago, but the King called me in, on a Sunday too. Something about burying an enemy of the state alive. I forget now—anyway, I missed the whole thing.'

'Well, let's get these chaps to put on a show. I'm sure they wouldn't mind,' the other guard said.

'Oh yeah, go on, let's see a bit of magic and clowning about—then you can use the loo!'

'Oh no, I'm sure you don't want to see us do our thing . . .' Santa said, glancing sideways at Jimmy.

'Yeah we do!' both guards replied. 'Let's get the other boys down here!'

The guard clicked the button on the side of his radio. 'This is alpha post. There's about to be a magic show, forward slash clown show, down here, in any second—any of you lads interested?'

'I couldn't!' Santa yelled. 'I . . . errrr . . . I don't have my big saw with me!'

'Oh, and Gavin, can you bring your biggest saw? Some bloke's about to slice an elf in half,' he said, smiling.

'How high are we?' Ben said, looking down.

'I've told you, don't look down!' Big Tony barked.

'You know, this goes against all kinds of health and safety regulations? I've got no hi-vis jacket, no helmet, and no ropes either. If I fall, it's goodbye Ben the 3D boy, and hello to my new life as a human pancake.'

'Oh, stop being such a child,' Big Tony sighed, taking another few feet up towards the roof.

'I am a child!' Ben bellowed. 'I should be in bed, snoring away, instead of breaking into a castle to deliver a bear.'

'Now listen, kid, you seem to have forgotten that you were actually responsible for Santa being so far behind. Trying to trap Santa like he was some sort of rabbit . . . You should be ashamed of yourself.' Big Tony shook his head.

'Yes, yes all right, but I think it's fair to say that I repaid that debt off some time ago.'

'You haven't repaid the debt until Big Tony says so!' Big Tony glared at Ben.

'Right, fine, let's keep going, but I must say your man-management skills leave a lot to be desired,' Ben huffed.

'Ok, how's about this? If you don't hurry up, I'll give you a smack in the chops,' Big Tony glowered.

'Fine! You see, was that so hard? It worked, look, I'm climbing higher and higher, quicker and quicker,' Ben said, simultaneously hurrying up and trying to escape.

'And now I've reached the top. You see, I did it,' Ben said sarcastically.

'I guess my man-management skills are pretty good after all,' Big Tony said, inching his way to the roof. 'Right, now according to my map, the kid's bedroom is directly below us. We slide down, deliver said bear, and get home in time for momma's famous *ragù*, sound good to you?'

'Great!' Ben said. 'Hand me the bear. After three . . .'

A crowd of a dozen or so guards had gathered outside the front of the castle. The good news was that Ben and Big Tony could deliver the bear uninterrupted. The bad news was the guards were waiting to see Santa cut Jimmy Knuckles in half.

'Well, this is a fine mess, isn't it?' Jimmy said, grimacing. "I'll do the old travelling circus scam, it'll be fine." You can't even remember that clowns don't do magic!'

'Shhh, it *will* be fine, just follow my lead.' Santa turned to the guards. 'Oh, what a beautiful saw!' he yelled loudly. 'It's so very sharp!'

'What are you going to do?' Jimmy said, looking at the steel teeth of the saw glinting at him.

'I'll start to cut you in half, then as soon as there's a spot of blood, I'll pretend to faint—you run into the woods, and I'll follow you in all the confusion.'

'What?! I don't like the sound of that one bit!' Jimmy hissed under his breath.

'Well, admittedly, running away isn't the greatest

plan, but it's all I've got at the moment.'

'Not that bit, the bit where you actually cut me in half.'

'I won't cut you in half, just slice a bit off—a bit you don't need.'

'I need all of me!' Jimmy yelled.

'Really? Are you sure?' Santa said, looking at Jimmy.

'Stop staring at my ears! Why are you staring at my ears?'

'Well, they are quite big. You do have a lot of ear for a small head. You look like a bat. I think you could easily lose a lobe and you'd be fine.'

'Hurry up!' one of the guards yelled.

'You've gone mad! Why should it be me anyway? What about you, chunky?'

'Who are you calling CHUNKY?!' Santa grabbed Jimmy. 'Don't worry, this is all part of the plan,' he whispered.

'It feels pretty real to me!' Jimmy whispered back, trying to get away. 'You look like you might want to cut my ears off.'

'They look quite angry,' one guard said. 'Why is the little one running away?'

THWACK! Jimmy kicked Santa in the shin and made a run for it.

'Is this part of the plan?' Santa whispered, 'I'm really confused and in a lot of pain.'

The guards looked at each other and began to chuckle. 'These guys are funny!'

THUD! Ben landed in the bedroom on his bottom. It really hurt, but not as much as Big Tony landing on his head a second later.

'Owowowow!' Ben said under his breath. He sat up and looked around the room. 'This can't be the place,' Ben said, scratching his head. 'There's no Prince Hector, just that sleeping bloke.' He pointed at the bed.

'That's Hector all right,' Big Tony said, making his way to a Christmas tree in the corner.

'How old is Hector?'

'He's nine,' Tony replied. 'Dump the bear, and let's get out of here.'

'Nine! He's as big as a rugby player.'

'He's just big-boned, that's all.'

'Big-boned? Look at him. He's bigger than Santa.'

At that moment, Prince Hector woke from his sleep. He snorted and huffed like a rhino in a boggy wetland.

'He's waking, quick, hide!' Ben yelled. He slid under the bed and waited for Hector to go back to sleep. But Hector didn't go back to sleep. There were two almighty thuds as the huge chunk of a child got out of bed and tiptoed as daintily as a T-rex in a heavy hat, towards the middle of the room.

'Oh golly gosh, Santa's been!' he squealed. Well, I say squealed; he honked like a ship's foghorn. Ben realized he was still holding the bear. But if he had the bear, what did Hector have? Ben pushed his head round the edge of the bed and looked up. There was Hector, cuddling Big Tony as though he was a Barbie doll. Big Tony was motionless, playing along with the notion that he was a toy.

'Oh no. He's going to crush him like a banana,' Ben muttered.

'Mummy and Daddy got Hector a new bear!' Hector skipped and danced around his bedroom. What was Ben going to do?

'Except, this isn't a cuddly little bear, this is a . . .' Suddenly Ben went very still. 'Say it . . . say it!'

'A cute little pixie!'

'PIXIE!' Big Tony broke out of character. 'Who are you calling a pixie, you huge lump of silly!'

'AAAAARRRGHHHH!' Hector cried, dropping Tony on his head.

Their cover was blown, but at least it meant they could try and escape. Ben rolled out from under the bed, grabbed Big Tony, and ran towards the door quickety-quick. He threw the presents towards the tree as he went, yelling 'MERRY CHRISTMAS!' before running out of the door.

Hector hit a large red button on the side of his bed, and a loud alarm rang around the whole castle.

Santa stopped running after Jimmy, the two of

them looked at each other and then at the castle. Santa looked at Jimmy, suddenly sheepish about the whole 'sawing-him-in-half-thing'.

'Let's never talk of this again,' Santa said. 'Sorry, Jimmy, it's been a long day.'

'You're right,' Jimmy cried back.

Big Tony and Ben came hurtling out of the front gates.

'RUUUUUUN. RUN AWAY!' yelled Ben; and Santa, Jimmy, and Big Tony all hurtled into the night. The guards didn't know what to make of it, and before they could do anything to stop them, a huge spotlight and a whirring sound descended from above.

'I didn't know the guards had helicopters!' Santa yelled.

'They don't!' Ben cried.

'THIS IS X SQUADRON. YOU ARE UNDER ARREST FOR COMMITTING INTERGALACTIC CRIMES AGAINST OUR PLANET. SURRENDER, OR PREPARE TO BE EXTERMINATED!'

# RUN RUDOLPH RUN

'To the Batmobile!' Santa cried.

'What?' Ben shouted.

'Just kidding, to the sleigh. I'm not Batman—I've just always wanted to say that.'

The helicopter swooped down to take up the chase, but the trees surrounding the castle were blocking their path.

'I can't get a clear sight of the aliens, boss,' Number 4 yelled into his radio. 'Too many obstacles.

I can see little men running away, though. Do we shoot on sight?'

'Hmmm, shoot on sight?' Number 1 repeated. 'No, I want this done by the book. We need them alive so they can take us back to their ship. Imagine how cool it would be to see a real UFO and capture it. We would be like the elite soldiers back at base. We'd probably get invited to all the coolest parties. People would want to be our friends . . . Yes, let's do that. We'll follow and capture their ship,' Number 1 squealed with excitement.

'Unless they fire on us again,' Number 2 chipped in.

'Oh yes, unless they fire at us again. If they do that, we'll just blast them out of the sky.'

'Look at the size of that gun!' Big Tony cried, craning his head to see the helicopter zipping over the trees, its spotlight trying to hunt them down. 'I'm scared, but also strangely attracted to it.'

The sleigh was parked about half a mile from the castle, a fair distance, but one easily manageable when there's someone chasing after you who wants you dead.

Fortunately, it was parked under the trees, which proved a vital cover. Santa leapt into the front driver's seat and the other three slotted in around him.

'I've got an idea,' Santa said. 'Everyone needs to hold on tight.'

'What?' Big Tony, Jimmy Knuckles, and Ben all answered back in unison.

'Hiyaaaaahh!' Santa yelled, cracking the reins. The reindeer galloped off faster than ever.

'I need your help, lads!' Santa cried, and the sleigh zoomed off into the sky almost vertically. Ben and the elves grabbed the buckles and strapped themselves in. Higher and higher the sleigh went, and soon they were higher than the mountains. Below them, the helicopter caught wind and started to follow.

'They're catching us!' Ben cried, but Santa didn't flinch. His gaze was steely and determined. Nothing was going to deter him from his plan. They were now higher than the clouds, and soon Ben could see the stars. It was like they were in space. Ben turned round—it was working—the helicopter seemed to be, dropping back.

'Number 1, we can't go any higher, soon the air will be too thin for the rotor blades to work,' Number 3 cried. The whole of the helicopter was flashing, and alarms of every sound and shape were going off. 'Sir, we need to drop back, it's too dangerous.'

Soon the sleigh peaked at the top of its climb, like a roller coaster before it rolls back down to earth.

'It worked, boss!' Big Tony smiled. 'But what now? We can't stay up here forever . . . Boss?'

Santa turned round and looked at them all. 'We need to get back to London; there's one last delivery to make, and we need to lose this helicopter, right?'

'Right,' Ben, Big Tony, and Jimmy answered.

'But how? Where can *we* go that a helicopter can't go?' Ben said, looking at the others.

'Helicopters don't go in tunnels.' Santa winked.

'Tunnels?' Ben scratched his head. 'But where's a tunnel around here . . .?'

Just at that second, the sleigh started its descent. 'We need to pick up as much speed as we can, it's the only way to out run them and get there first,' Santa yelled.

'Oh no . . .!' Ben said, realizing suddenly what the plan was.

'What?!' Big Tony and Jimmy cried together.

'Santa, no, are you insane? What if there's a train running?' Ben shouted.

'It's Christmas Eve, there probably won't be,' Santa replied.

'Probably?!' Ben cried.

'Will someone tell us what's going on!' Big Tony demanded.

'Santa's going to fly us into England through the channel tunnel, from way up here. Getting the sleigh, the reindeer and us through all at once is like trying to thread a needle by jumping off a ladder—it's madness!' Ben yelled.

'Exciting though!' Santa cried, as he slipped his goggles over his eyes. 'Hold on, everyone.'

Ben, Big Tony, and Jimmy yelled like kids on the big dipper as the sleigh plummeted over Transilmania towards the northern coast of France.

'This will never work, what's the matter with you?' Ben shrieked.

'Listen,' Santa yelled, 'I don't know who these guys are, or why they're after us, but we've got a job to do.'

'They're coming back down to earth, Number 1,' Number 3 yelled.

'Good, follow them!' Number 1 barked.

'I don't think we can. They have incredible speed—I think they're aiming for the channel tunnel. I think this might be an attack.'

Number 1 looked at the radar.

'Sir, what do we do? Do we let them go, or do we take them out?' Number 2 asked, his voice filled with fear for the first time.

Number 1 just stared ahead. He'd never been this close to an Unidentified Flying Object, and he might never get this close again. Should he risk capturing it, or end it all now to avoid an attack?

'Sir,' Number 2 said, grabbing his hands, 'it's now or never.'

'OK, let's do it,' Number 1 said. 'Fire up the missile, let's make this a clean takedown. No mess.'

'Sir, yes sir.' The other three saluted.

The sleigh hurtled towards Northern France, aiming straight for the tunnel.

'Are you definitely sure there are no trains running today?' Ben asked.

'It's Christmas Eve; who works on Christmas Eve?!' Santa yelled. His eyes were wide with excitement, like a kid going down a really steep slide for the first time.

'Well, we do for a start. Why did we have to come up so high in order reach the tunnel, anyway?' Ben said, picking the bugs out of his teeth.

'I thought it'd be more fun,' Santa smiled.

'More fun?!'

'Christmas is about having fun, isn't it?' Santa said. 'In fact, who fancies a sing-song?'

'What?' Ben, Big Tony, and Jimmy screamed.

'We're plunging towards earth at about 200 mph,

to fly into a concrete tunnel, powered by animals, driven by, and no offence, a man recovering from a head injury, who wants us all to have a nice little carol service while we do it?!'

'What's your point?'

'It's a good job you weren't captain of the *Titanic*. You'd have us playing a game of pin the tail on the donkey, instead of climbing into those pesky life-boats,' Ben spluttered.

'Is that a "no" to the sing-song?' Santa asked.

'YES!' the other three yelled.

'Oh well, we're here now anyway, so I guess we don't have time.'

In the distance, Ben could see the entrance to the tunnel. The railway lines looked deserted—but for how long?

'All I will say . . .' Santa added, 'is keep your hands and feet inside the sleigh at all times.'

'FIRE!' Number 3 cried out, before hitting a button on his joystick. The helicopter fired one of its many missiles straight at the sleigh. It exploded like an angry firework, hissing and snaking through the air.

Ben looked over his shoulder at the missile hurtling towards them. It didn't matter how fast they were flying, this helicopter was relentless. Ben closed his eyes and held his breath as the sleigh darted into the tunnel. The missile missed by a whisker, and blew up a nearby supermarket, which was, thankfully, closed and deserted.

'Damage report, Number 2?'

'There has been quite a lot of damage,' Number 2 replied.

'Sir, sir, just before the UFO disappeared into the tunnel, my radar picked up something. It sounded like a primitive language, like the one I heard before. Perhaps that's how they communicate?'

'What did it say?' Number 1 asked.

'Listen for yourself,' Number 3 replied. There was a crackle and the sound of some shouting.

'I'M GONNAAAAAAAAAAAAAA DOOOOOO A TROOOOOUSER BURRRRRRP!'

Everyone looked at each other. 'Did . . . anyone else hear that? I mean, I know what I think it sounded like, but did anyone else hear the bit about . . .?' Number 3 asked.

'Doing a trouser burp? Yes, yes we all did,' Number 2 replied.

'Where does this train line go to?' Number 1 yelled. 'Take us there, now!'

# SANTA CLAUS IS COMING TO TOWN

'The train now arriving at St Pancras is . . . *not* the overnight Eurostar from Paris. It looks more like a sleigh and some pixies . . .' the station speakers announced.

'Right, that's it! The next person who calls me a pixie is going to get a little *elf* visit in the middle of the night,' Big Tony growled as the sleigh came sliding up the track to a stop on the platform.

'Oh leave it, Tony, it's really not worth it,' Santa urged. 'And who knew that a sleigh would fit perfectly on the tracks. We should go by rail more often.'

Santa yanked the reins once more and the sleigh flew up from the rails and over the barriers, into London's breaking dawn. It had snowed while they'd been travelling round the world, but now it had stopped, the dusting made London look like a toy town—the snow sparkling and twinkling in the early light.

'We're nearly done, Ben, and then we can get you home and get these two back for a nap.' Santa smiled as the sleigh swished over the Victorian roof-tops, spires, and many chimneys that gave London its Tetris skyline.

'There's no sign of that helicopter, but let's not hang about, just in case. The sun's almost up and we need to make our last delivery before we can go home.'

'Well that's a very serious question, Dave.'

'I know, Keith, that's why I asked you.'

'It's not something you can just blurt out. It needs time, thought, and consideration.'

'I know, Keith.'

In a lay-by next to a deserted road sat a police car, where Dave and Keith, two unlucky PCs who found themselves on duty on Christmas Day, were deep in conversation.

'Top three Keith.'

'Top three Dave.'

'Right then, Keith, if I had to choose, right here right now, I'd say my top three cheeses in descending order were parmesan, brie, and cheddar.'

'SHUT UP! Cheddar at number 3? What's the matter with you?'

'I'm sorry, but yes, cheddar comes third. It is tasty, but does it bring my pasta to life the way parmesan does? No.'

'Well Dave, I tell you, I'm shocked, I thought stilton was as daring as you might go, but never this. I thought we knew each other, and then you go and drop a brie bomb on me like this.'

'What shall we play now, Keith?' Dave said looking out of the window. There was not a soul about. The two policemen hadn't seen anything for hours. The sun was beginning to come up and there were a few snowflakes dancing around in the air.

'Top three Quality Street?'

'Nah,' Keith answered. 'That's a minefield. I did that one with my last partner, Big Bob, you know Big Bob? Big fella, called Bob—you know?'

'I know.'

'Well, we did the Quality Street question, and it was all going fine until I mentioned the blue coconut eclair, and, I kid you not, he came at me with a traffic cone. Not one of those little ones either, a big cone. Well, he got kicked out of the force after that. So no Quality Street stuff, it's a dangerous road to go down, let me tell you.'

'Blimey, I had no idea. What does he do now?' Dave asked.

'Primary School teacher.'

'Wow.'

'Yep.'

'So what then, Keith, what shall we play— hide and seek?' Dave suggested looking out of the window. 'Looks awfully chilly actually, maybe not.'

'Oh I know—snooker!' Keith said, smiling.

'Snooker? Oh Keith, I think you might have gone quite mad! Snooker, in a car?!'

'Not real snooker, car snooker. We sit here and wait for a red car to go past, then we pull them over, make up some excuse about why, wish them a Merry Christmas and send them on their way. Then we wait for a yellow, green, brown, blue, pink, and then a black car to pull over. We can see how many points we score.'

'Brilliant, Keith! So we need a red one first, then a different colour, but black gets the most points?'

'Yep!'

Just at that very moment, Father Christmas's sleigh zipped overhead, its red paint gleaming in the half-light.

'Red!' Dave and Keith yelled at once. And then a helicopter zoomed over too.

Dave and Keith looked at each other, 'BLACK!' they both cried. Dave threw the rest of his tea out of the window and Keith started up the engine.

'Woo-wahs?' Dave asked Keith.

'Oh yeah, woo-wahs,' Keith answered, and with

that, Dave hit the lights and sirens, and the air was suddenly punctuated with the screaming sound of 'WOOOOO-WAAAAAAAAAH!' as the car sped in pursuit of the sleigh and helicopter.

'We've got them, Number 1, this time there's nowhere to hide,' Number 2 cried.

'Oh dear, oh dear, oh dear,' Santa sighed. 'Looks like we've got company again—the helicopter *and* the police are after us now. Oh dear, oh dear.'

'Right, so what's the plan?' asked Ben.

'I don't know.' Santa looked nervously back at Ben. 'The trouble is, I've run out of plans.'

'But you always have a plan!' Ben cried, seeing the police car below and the helicopter up high. 'Let's just out run them.'

'I can't do that. The reindeer have been running all night. They don't have it in them.'

'Wait a second, I know this place! We're near where I live,' Ben said looking around.

'Ah yes, one more house left to do,' Santa smiled.

'You mean my house?' Ben yelled. 'Forget my house—just drop me somewhere and get out of here.'

'A promise is a promise!' Santa smiled back.

'Don't worry about me—just make sure you and the elves are safe.'

'No can do,' Santa replied.

'I forbid you to turn down my road!' Ben cried, as the sleigh turned down his road. 'Oh no, my Mum's going to be furious,' Ben sighed.

Ben's house came into view at alarming speed. Father Christmas was coming in too fast, and the sleigh skidded and bounced off the roof before coming to a screeching halt, with inches to spare.

Ben looked round. He could hear the sirens of the police car and he could see the dark shadow of the helicopter. This was madness, they were never going to escape, what was Santa thinking?

'Big Tony, Jimmy Knuckles, you two stay here and watch the sleigh,' Santa said.

'Oh thank goodness,' Big Tony sighed with relief, snuggling down.

'I said keep watch!' Santa said shaking his head. 'Not cat-nap! Bloomin' elves. Come on lad, let's get this over and done with, the sun's almost up. Any later and we're in the awake zone.'

Ben and Santa jumped down the chimney. The familiar whooshing and squeezing still made Ben squirm and giggle. The two of them landed with a quiet thud on the floor, where the whole night had started. Santa opened up the sack and placed it by the tree. Suddenly there was a flash of light from outside ,and then the familiar rumblings of chopper blades and two more thuds as Big Tony and Jimmy came flying down the chimney after Santa and Ben.

'Helicopter!' Big Tony yelled pointing towards

the window. Suddenly the door of the living room came crashing in.

'No one move!' a voice bellowed.

'Get down, all of you!' another voice yelled.

Ben and Santa hit the deck.

'Please don't shoot!' Ben cried. 'We're just here to deliver a few presents!'

'Presents?' Dave piped up, 'Ooh, I love presents!'

Suddenly the lights came on. It took a second for Ben's eyes to adjust. Two policemen were standing in his living room.

'I thought you were breaking in and stealing stuff, but instead you're breaking in and giving presents,' the other policeman smiled. 'But breaking in is still wrong, so I'm afraid you're both under arrest.'

Just at that moment, a team of four soldiers dressed in black came crashing through the window. 'Stop in the name of the law!' one yelled, his face covered by a balaclava.

'Oh for goodness' sake!' Keith cried. 'Who are you lot? You really should take some flying lessons.'

'My name's Number 1.'

'Number 1, what . . . did you have weird parents?' Dave asked, scratching his head. 'I went to a school with a boy called Crispin Wibbly. I never met his parents, but I imagined they were probably a bit odd. Mind you, if your name's Wibbly, there's probably not many names that sound good in front of it.'

'No,' Number 1 said, 'My parents are fine, I mean, my Mum and Dad are fine, I mean, that's my code name, you know, so no one knows who I am.'

'Oooh, I see, yes, very clever, and you're here because?' Keith asked.

'We're here chasing a UFO and I believe these men are aliens,' he said, pointing at Ben and Santa.

'Aliens?!' Ben, Santa, and the elves all yelled together.

'What?' Dave interrupted. 'These are humans! I mean, look at this one's beard, it's as human as it gets.'

'It's definitely an alien. Look, this beard is probably a disguise.' Number 1 ran over and yanked at Santa's beard, trying to pull it off.

'Ouch!' Santa cried.

'No, it can't be!' Number 1 cried. 'I've been chasing what I thought was an alien across the world, and it wasn't an alien at all,' Number 1 whimpered.

'Well, we all have bad days,' Big Tony offered.

'No, no, I tried to shoot you down,' Number 1 sobbed. 'You're not an alien, you're . . .' Number 1 pulled off his balaclava.

'DAD!' Ben cried.

There was silence for a second. Numbers 2, 3, and 4 looked at each other, and pulled off their balaclavas too. Big Tony looked at Jimmy, and Jimmy at Santa.

'Well, this is awkward . . .' Dave said, looking at his feet.

'I thought you were away on business,' Ben yelled. 'Why are you not on business?'

'I am!' Number 1 cried, 'This is my business. Son, I don't know how to tell you this, but I'm not who you think I am.' Number 1 shook his head.

'To be honest, I don't really know what you do anyway. I mean I'm not really sure what it was you pretended to do.'

'Son, I work for the army, tracking down and trying to capture aliens,' Ben's dad said, looking very sheepish. 'I'm so sorry, I should have told you.'

'But why are you away every Christmas?'

'Christmas is the time when most UFO sightings are seen. It goes mad this time of year, I don't know why.'

Ben's dad took another look around the room, his gaze finally resting on Santa. 'Oh right, that's why . . .' he sighed, realizing that in fact he'd probably just been seeing Santa's sleigh each year.

'I missed you,' Ben said, feeling both cross and sad at the same time.

'I never really liked Christmas, to be honest,' Ben's dad huffed.

'But it's CHRISTMAS!' Ben looked horrified.

'I never liked it . . .'

'What?!' Big Tony yelled. 'Hey Santa, do you want me to take this guy outside and teach him a few manners, elf style?' Tony hit his hand into his other hand and sneered.

'I'm sorry, I'm sorry, but all I ever wanted that one Christmas was a toy UFO!' Number 1 sank to his knees and began to sob.

'Oh no, he's crying,' Dave said to Keith. 'When did we become a nation of criers? What's wrong with bottling it all up?'

'Crying is good for you, ignore him Number 1,' Number 2 smiled.

'I just wanted my toy,' Number 1 wept.

'There, there,' Santa smiled. 'I'm sorry, Number 1—I mean Derek—sometimes things get lost, but I always get there in the end.'

Santa reached into his bag. 'I found this in the back of the sleigh. I didn't realize it had been lost for so long. That's what I was doing at your house Ben, bringing your dad his present.'

'Derek . . .?' Number 2 said, looking at the others. 'I knew Number 1 wasn't his real name, but Derek?'

Ben's dad tore the wrapping paper off in double-quick time. 'It's my own UFO!' he cried.

'Awwwww,' the rest of the room all said together.

'There is just one more thing I'd like . . .?' Ben's Dad smiled. 'I mean, if you have time.'

# SIMPLY HAVING A
# WONDERFUL CHRISTMAS TIME

'Well this is the best way to spend Christmas ever, riding around on a UFO! Faster, make it go faster!' Ben's dad squealed.

'It's not a UFO, Dad, it's a sleigh.' Ben shook his head.

'It's a very cramped sleigh,' Big Tony sniffed.

'You should try being down here,' came the muffled yell of Jimmy Knuckles.

'It's been quite a night,' Ben said. 'I've been around the world, chased through the channel tunnel, and met a prince.' Ben turned to his dad. 'What will you do now that you've found out little green men don't exist

. . . Well, apart from elves.'

'I dunno. I guess I might leave the army—there doesn't seem much point chasing UFOs any more, and I don't really like fighting people, so it's probably best if I find another job. I've always liked the idea of opening a little shop. One that sells sweets.'

'Yes!' Ben cried. 'Best day ever. I get my dad back and he buys a sweet shop.' Ben fist bumped himself.

'I'm really sorry I wasn't around more,' Ben's dad said, clutching Ben's hand. 'I just got caught up, thinking that work was more important than anything else. I think it's fair to say I've learnt my lesson. No more flying around—well, apart from now I mean. From now on I think we should spend more time together. We've got a lot to catch up on.'

'OK, if you say so,' came the muffled reply from under Big Tony.

'I think he was talking to me, Jimmy,' Ben replied.

'Did you really capture Santa?' Ben's dad asked.

'Yep.' Ben smiled.

'Wow, I've been trying for years to catch him, back when I thought he was an alien, but I never got close.

You clearly have talent!' Ben's dad said, holding his hand.

'We're nearly back,' Santa said. 'I bet your mum will be wondering where you are.'

'I doubt it,' Ben's dad said. 'She'll be fast asleep.'

'An earthquake couldn't wake her up,' Ben laughed.

'Well, she might wake up when I tell her I'm leaving the army to sell liquorice laces.' Dad smiled.

'Here we are.' Santa brought the sleigh down to land in the middle of the street. There was just enough snow for the skis to have a soft and quiet landing.

'Well, goodbye Big Tony, and to you, Jimmy.' Ben offered his hand, but it was too late, both elves were fast asleep. 'Ah, best not to wake them.'

'Thanks, Santa. And thanks for the present, it means a lot—oh and sorry for trying to kill you. I do feel bad about that.' Ben's dad held out his hand to shake.

'I'm a hugger!' Santa smiled, giving Ben's dad a

big, squeezy hug.

'I'll go and open the door,' Ben's dad said, strolling up the path.

'Thanks, Santa.' Ben smiled.

'Thank you, lad. I wouldn't have made this year's Christmas run if it wasn't for you. And that wouldn't do at all,' Santa said, giving Ben a big hug too.

'Well, I did nearly kill you myself, so it's the least I could do. I promise no one else in my family will try and do away with you ever again.'

'Well, that's a relief. I don't think the world's ready for Big Tony to be Santa quite yet,' Father Christmas chuckled. 'But if you and your dad fancy a ride next year, just write!'

'Wow, really?! Oh that'd be so cool,' Ben grinned.

'And there's always a job for you here, you know. You've got a natural talent. I could do with someone to train the elves. And I won't be around forever. I'll need someone to take hold of the reins one day, literally!'

'Thanks, Father Christmas, but I think I'm just going to have a normal few Christmases for now.

I think there are a few that my Dad and I have missed out on.' Ben smiled.

Santa got back into his sleigh and waved at Ben. With a last pull on the reins, the reindeer and the two snoozing elves glided off into the night. Ben waved until he couldn't see them any more, and headed inside.

'It's just occurred to me,' Ben's dad said, scratching his head. 'Did Santa give you a present?'

'I wasn't expecting one,' Ben said. He had his dad, which is what he asked for, after all.

'Well, this must be for you.' Ben's dad smiled and handed Ben a rectangular present, neatly wrapped with his name on it.

'What is it?' Ben asked.

'I don't know; it's not from me or your mum. I guess there's one way to find out.'

Ben pulled off the wrapping paper. There was a neat photo frame and inside it was the blurred picture of Santa that Ben had taken with his mum's polaroid camera. Santa must have put it in a frame when he wasn't looking.

'It's Santa! There's a message too,' Ben said, bringing it closer to get a better view.

'What does it say?'

'It says, "*To Ben, I hope you have a great Christmas with your Dad. P.S. Of course I got your letter xxx*" . . .' Ben's voice trailed off. 'I don't understand.'

'Do you think,' Ben's dad asked, 'that this was his plan all along? That he faked not knowing who he was, all just so we could end up spending Christmas together?'

'Morning!' Mum walked into the living room. 'Derek, what are you doing here? Ben, you look like you've been up all night!'

'Mum, the most incredible thing happened. You'll never guess who I met!' Ben laughed.

'Who?' Mum said.

'Come and look, darling,' Ben's Dad said, pointing towards the window. There in the distance, the sleigh shot across the sky. The lights on it flashed, writing Happy Christmas in the sky as it weaved between the stars.

'Oh my crikey!' she yelled. 'ALIENS!'

ALSO BY **Tom McLaughlin**

# I DON'T LIKE MONDAYS

'**B**LEEEEEEEEEEEP!'

There are many awful sounds in this world. Fingernails down the blackboard, Mum singing the theme tune to Match of the Day in the shower, bagpipes being played badly, in fact bagpipes being played brilliantly as well. But there are none worse than the sound of an alarm clock early on a Monday.

'Why are mornings so early?' Joe muttered to himself, before trying to grab his alarm clock, missing it and falling out of bed. This was not uncommon for Joe.

He often fell, even when no falling was required. He was one of life's great fallers. He fell into rooms, he fell out of them again. He even managed the almost impossible task of falling upstairs which, let me tell you, is no mean feat. Joe's life was a constant battle with gravity, one in which gravity clearly had the upper hand. He picked himself up from the bedroom floor and set about trying to get dressed without opening his eyes. It was a trick that he tried to help fool his sleepy head that he was still in bed. The downside was it made putting pants on very tricky indeed. Up to that point, putting on underwear with his eyes shut was as close to living on the edge as Joe's life got.

Joe lived in a tiny house in London with his mum. Dad had disappeared before Joe was born and he didn't have any brothers or sisters. The nearest he ever came to having a sibling was the time when a cat from down the street came to stay for ten days last year. Other than Mr Tiddles, it had only ever been the two of them. Joe's mum was a park warden, and that meant she spent most of her days making sure that the flowers were looked after and no dogs were doing their doings where they shouldn't.

It was a job she loved, and Joe loved her working there too. Joe's house didn't have a garden, just a tiny yard, the sort of place where you'd graze your knee if you fell over. Which as you know, is something Joe did a lot. So the park always felt like his and Mum's garden. When Mum wasn't in the park, pruning flowers and shouting at dog owners, she was in the kitchen cooking. It was her thing. She would stop off at the shops and buy the bags of food that no one else wanted, which she'd use for inspiration in the kitchen, thinking up extraordinarily weird recipes with which to torture . . . I mean impress, Joe. Joe knew that it was really because money was sometimes tight, but it meant that meal times were never dull—I mean, who can forget the cheese salad with onion gravy, or the plum tandoori crumble? Apart from the odd, odd meal, Joe's life was pretty unremarkable. Apart from . . .

# BRRRRIIIIIIIING!

Just then the doorbell rang.

'LET ME IN, IT'S AN EMERGENCY!' came the exasperated cry from the other side.

Joe's mum opened the door and there stood Ajay, Joe's oldest and best friend.

'What is it, Ajay?' Joe's mum said, sounding panic-stricken.

'I smell your world-famous fresh tea and toast with sour rhubarb jam, Mrs P, and I need a fix!' Ajay grinned and waggled an eyebrow up and down. Ajay was the only person in the world who found Joe's mum's cooking not only edible, but enjoyable too. Then again, Ajay did once eat a fingerful of his own earwax in Geography for a bet, so it's fair to say he probably hasn't got the most sophisticated palate.

'Oh, Ajay, doesn't your mother feed you?' Joe's mum asked, rolling her eyes. But she was well used to Ajay's tardis-like stomach.

'Breakfast is the most important meal of the day, Mrs P, that's why I make it my business to have as many as possible. Got any pork pies?' Ajay grinned, pushing past her in the direction of the breakfast table.

'You know I hate those things, Ajay!' Mum said, shaking her head. 'I think it's the jelly—it makes me squeamish.'

Ajay and Joe had been friends since they were at nursery when they found out they had the same birthday. And let me tell you, when you're three, that sort of thing blows your mind, which pretty much means you're destined to be bestest friends for life. If it wasn't for Ajay, school would be nothing more than a yawn factory. Ajay was the sort of boy who made even the dullest, dreariest things in life seem a giggle. He was always scheming, always thinking of a plan to make the teacher laugh. Or trying to figure out how they were both going to become millionaires by next Tuesday. These plans nearly always involved Joe and nearly always failed—but that was half the fun.

Ajay was just about to tuck into his tea and toast dripping in sour rhubarb jam when there was a loud clatter from the letterbox as an important-looking brown envelope landed on the mat.

'Bit early for the post isn't it?' Mum said. 'Ooh, it says Special Delivery.' She opened it, and unfolded the letter.

Joe knew instantly that something was wrong. He could see it on Mum's face.

'What is it, Mum?' Joe asked.

'Yeah, Mrs P, what's happened?' Ajay asked too.

'It's the park . . . they've shut it down.'

For a second no one said a word. Joe and Ajay looked at each other, then back at Joe's mum. Her face was pale, her jaw dropped open. She stared at the letter, her eyes watery and ready to spill over with tears.

'Shut the park!' Joe said furiously. 'They can't do that, it's . . . it's the park!'

'Yeah, everyone loves that place!' Ajay joined in.

'You boys best get to school, or you'll be late,' said Mum, her voice all shaky.

'But what about . . . ?' Joe started to say.

'You leave that to me, I don't want you worrying.' Mum tried to smile, but it didn't reach her eyes. If she was trying to reassure Joe, it wasn't working. He knew his mum needed that job—how else was she supposed to put sweet-and-sour spaghetti on the table?

'Don't worry, Mum, I'll . . . I'll think of something.'

Joe's mum just nodded, turning away to wipe her eyes.

Joe and Ajay grabbed their bags and reluctantly headed out of the door. Neither of them said anything for what seemed like ages.

'You all right, man?' Ajay asked, breaking the silence.

'I don't know . . . I can't believe they've closed the park. I mean, why?!' Joe said in disbelief.

'Dunno,' Ajay shrugged. 'But I know a man who might,' he said, pointing down the road.

As they turned the corner at the top of Joe's street they saw a man in the distance. He had a ladder and toolbox and was busy hammering a sign into the park gates. This made Joe's blood boil. If Mum had been there she would have given him what for—no one hammers anything into anything without her say-so first.

'Oi!' Ajay yelled, 'what are you doing?'

Joe read the sign: 'Under development.'

'What's going on?' Joe asked. 'Why have you closed the park?'

The man stopped what he was doing and shrugged. 'They don't tell me anything—I'm just the bloke who hammers things.'

Joe read the rest of the sign.

UNDER DEVELOPMENT
'THIS NOTICE HEREBY DECLARES THAT ST GEORGE'S PARK IS CLOSED WITH IMMEDIATE EFFECT AND THAT FROM 1ST OF JULY, THIS PARK WILL BE REDEVELOPED AND A NEW BLOCK OF LUXURY FLATS WILL BE BUILT—DEPARTMENT OF PROGRESS'

Underneath the notice was a drawing of a posh building, tall and made of glass. It had pictures of smiling people chatting and drinking coffee outside. Joe and Ajay looked through the park gates and could already see diggers moving in, ready to tear the playground apart.

'This can't be happening,' Joe muttered, blinking back the tears. This was the place where he and Ajay hung out. Where they used to plot how they were going to become mega rich, and plan what to do if the world got taken over by zombies. This was the place where Joe and Ajay used to play football—or rather where Ajay would kick the ball and Joe would try to get out of the way of it before it hit him in the face. And now it was going to be turned into flats! Why wasn't anyone stopping this?

''Ello 'ello, anything I can do?'

Joe turned to see a policeman, standing by the sign and looking down at Joe and Ajay.

'Yes!' Joe gasped. 'Stop this man from closing the park!'

'Yes officer,' Ajay joined in, 'arrest this man.'

'Eh?' said the man hammering. 'What did *I* do?'

'You're closing the park!' Ajay yelled at him.

'I told you, I'm just the bloke who does the hammering, I'm not closing anything.'

Just then, a group of police motorcycle outriders whizzed past, sirens screaming and lights flashing as they went. It was like something from a movie, only it was happening in their street.

'What on earth!' the man on the ladder said, nearly but, rather disappointingly, not falling off.

'Ooooh!' said Ajay, glaring wide-eyed at the convoy of flashing blue lights and sirens. 'Do you think there's been a bank robbery? Or maybe aliens have landed!'

'Oh, I hope it's an alien invasion!' said Joe. 'We'd definitely get the day off school for that.'

'It's the Prime Minister,' said the policeman. 'He's visiting here today and I'm here as back-up.'

'You mean you're not here to stop them closing the park?' Joe said.

'Oh no, looks like the park's had it,' he said, peering at the sign. 'Shame, I used to play here as a kid.'

'Where is the Prime Minister visiting?' Joe asked.

'A school I think . . . Yes, it's definitely a school.'

There was only one school down that end of the road. Joe and Ajay's school. Ajay and Joe looked at each other and, without saying a word, they grabbed their bags and ran. Well, Ajay ran, Joe tripped over his laces.

'I bet he can save the park!' Joe yelled, picking himself up.

'Bound to!' Ajay grinned. 'At the very least we'll probably get out of double Algebra!'

'This is even better than the time that dog came in the playground and pooed on the netball court!' yelled Joe.

'Well, I don't know, that was a pretty special day,' said Ajay seriously, 'but it's definitely up there.'

By the time Ajay and Joe got to school there was a huge crowd already there, of excited schoolchildren, policemen, TV reporters, and cross-looking members of the public. There, at the front of the crowd, stood the headmaster, Mr Brooks.

Ajay nudged Joe. 'Mr Brooks looks . . . well, really weird. Has he combed his hair differently?'

Mr Brooks had indeed combed his hair, but that wasn't it. Suddenly Joe figured it out.

'I know, I know! He's smiling!'

'Oh yeah,' Ajay realized. 'It's really creepy, isn't it?'

'What's going on, Mr Brooks?' said Joe.

Mr Brooks sighed impatiently. 'Oh no, not you two! I warn you—any mischief and you'll be for the high jump!'

'Is the Prime Minister coming, sir?' Ajay asked, looking at the big black limo that had just pulled up behind the police motorcycles.

'Yes. It was supposed to be a secret, you know, for security reasons, seeing as how he's pretty much hated by most people these days. But some buffoon must have told the papers. I mean, look at all these cameras!' he said, suddenly grinning and running a licked finger over one eyebrow.

The doors of the black limo opened and out stepped a stout man in a mud-coloured suit. He had a red, wobbly face, in the middle of which sat a bulbous nose, like a cherry on a particularly disgusting trifle. The man dabbed his sweaty face with a hanky and attempted to flatten his wispy hair with a clammy hand.

The man in question was Percival T. Duckholm. He was the Prime Minister of Great Britain and, it's fair to say, one of the most disliked men in the land. He was the kind of man who would not only sell his grandmother for a quick buck, but he'd also try to sell your grandmother too. In fact, if you've got a moment I suggest you give her a quick ring and tell her not to answer the door to any trifle-faced Prime Ministers. Percival T. Duckholm was also one of the rudest men you're ever likely to meet. He liked to shout at people—in fact, shouting was his most favourite thing in the world. He'd shout in the morning at breakfast to his poor wife and pale children. Then he'd have a bath and shout a bit in there.

Then he'd get dressed and shout about how he couldn't find his socks, then he'd go to work and shouty-shout-shout until lunch, before it all got too much and he had to have a nap until it was home time.

You may well say, surely he can't be this bad? Surely someone must like him—I mean, he did manage to become Prime Minister after all? Well, the simple truth is the man he was up against was even more loathsome. I know, it's hard to believe. But let me tell you about Melvyn Thwick, a man so obnoxious that if you ever got to meet him it would take all your strength not to vomit through your nose just to be in the same room as him. He had greasy hair, terrible breath and dandruff so bad, you'd think winter had come early by looking at the state of his shoulders. He picked his nose with all the eagerness and desperation of a man looking for loose change down the back of the sofa. When he spoke he sounded like farts. He had the charm and manners of a drunk pig feeding at the trough. He hated pretty much anyone and everything and he made no secret of trying to hide it. So it's not hard to see why he chose a career in politics.

So there you have it, that's the very short story of

Percival T. Duckholm's rise to power: he just happened to find an opponent that was even more repulsive than him. So anyway, where were we? Oh yes, Percival T. Duckholm emerged from the car. He waved and smiled at the crowds, even though no one was cheering him. In fact they were booing him. Joe looked round and saw that quite a mob had gathered. The more Percival smiled, the more they shouted and wailed at him.

'Resign, you lump!' one angry lady yelled.

'You're a crook!' another man shouted.

This just seemed to whip the reporters and cameramen into more of a frenzy. Pervical T. Duckholm ignored the crowd and headed for Mr Brooks.

'What a marvellous school you have here!' he said.

'Thank you. Would you like to meet some of the children?' Mr Brooks replied, eagerly.

'God no. It's bad enough that I have to spend time with my own!'

Joe pushed his way to the front of the crowd. This was his chance—he figured that if he just explained about the park to the Prime Minister, he would fix it—I mean, that's what Prime Ministers do, isn't it? They fix things.

'Er . . . Mr Prime Minister, sir, can I ask you a question?' Joe asked timidly.

'EW!' the PM shrieked. 'GET AWAY FROM ME YOU 'ORRIBLE CREATURE!'

'I just wanted to ask you a question—it's about our park . . .'

'You just wanted to fart a question about a parp?' the Prime Minister asked. 'Speak up, boy!'

'No, I wanted to ask a question about the park. Our park has been closed down, and they're going to build a big shiny tower on it.' By now, everyone was listening. Even Mr Brooks was staring at Joe, a mixture of bewilderment and anger on his face (mostly anger, maybe five per cent bewilderment). Joe wasn't used to people actually listening to him. He normally liked to sit quietly and let Ajay take the lead, but he knew this could be his only chance to save his mum's job.

'Ahhhh . . .' the Prime Minister said, smiling. 'At last, a sensible question. Yes it's true, we have closed down the grotty old park and built a shiny new tower. That's what this government is all about, building shiny new things. No need to thank me, sonny Jim!'

the PM gave Joe a toothy grin, ruffled his hair and walked away.

'What an idiot,' Ajay said, looking at the Prime Minister. 'Hey Joe, are you all right?'

But Joe wasn't all right. He was about a zillion miles from all right. His blood was hot and full of anger. How could someone so important be so useless? He felt like a fly that had just been swatted to the floor. The Prime Minister moved on, surrounded by reporters and cameramen. They were like a pack of animals, feeding on every word that fell out of his greasy mouth.

'Charlie James, World News Today. Do you have anything to say for yourself? Anything at all about the allegations that you're a crook and a thief?'

'NO COMMENT!' Percival bellowed like a fog horn in a storm.

'Do we take it from your silence that the crimes they accuse you of are true, Prime Minister?'

'Now listen here, you horrible little man!'

'Are insults the best you can do, Prime Minister?' Charlie asked, shoving the microphone right into the PM's face.

Percival T. Duckholm, clearly having had enough of being pestered, stopped in his tracks and whipped round to face the reporter.

'I know in recent days there have been several accusations about me in the newspapers. Well, I would like to say once and for all, I deny any wrong-doing. I can assure you that the huge amount of money the police found in my bank account was simply resting there until I had time to give it to the home for orphaned kittens. Furthermore, I can assure you that it was a genuine mix-up when I accidentally sold my grandmother to that travelling circus. I would also like to deny that it was me caught on camera giving those bags of cash to those dodgy businessmen—it was in fact my twin brother, that I only just discovered I had last week.

NOW GO AWAY!'

The sound of jeering and booing rose a level. The Prime Minister's pink sweat-glazed face was getting more and more irate-looking with every passing moment.

'What about the Deputy Prime Minister, Violetta Crump—do you still stand by her?' the news reporter asked. But before the Prime Minister had a chance to answer, another voice interrupted.

'Let me answer that.'

Out of the car stepped a woman dressed from head to toe in black. Her painted nails flashed in the sunlight like knives at the ends of her hands. This was Violetta Crump, the Deputy Prime Minister. She was a chilling woman, with brains as sharp as a pot of pencils dipped in lemon juice. She had a steely look on her face that made everyone feel puny and unimportant and her eyes were sly, like a snake's. The angry people were all now looking nervously at their feet, quivering.

'Do you still support the Prime Minister, Ms Crump?' Charlie James asked, his voice wobbling with fright.

'The Prime Minister and I go back a long way. He's like family to me—and one I like, not one I'd sell to a circus.'

Percival laughed nervously.

'There have been many accusations about the Prime Minister in the last few days, but I don't know why anyone would think it was *me* who told the papers about the Prime Minister's crimes—I'm sorry, his *alleged* crimes. All this talk that I'm after his job is just that, talk. Why would I want Percy's job? His big house, his power? Oh no, I'm just happy to work for such a . . . special man.' Violetta looked at Percival T. Duckholm as if he were a slug stuck on her shoe.

'Well there you have it. Violetta thinks I'm brilliant. I think I'm brilliant, now let's put this silly matter to rest. I am in charge of you lot and there's not a single thing you can do about it!'

'Oh, will you shut up, you bumbling great warthog!' came a small voice from the crowd. Mr Brooks looked round, Charlie James looked round, Violetta looked round, Ajay looked round . . . and there stood Joe, his arms folded crossly, staring at Percival T. Duckholm. There was a deathly hush.

# ABOUT THE AUTHOR

Before becoming a writer and illustrator Tom spent nine years working as political cartoonist for *The Western Morning News* thinking up silly jokes about even sillier politicians. Then, in 2004 Tom took the plunge into illustrating and writing his own books. Since then he has written and illustrated picture books as well as working on animated TV shows for Disney and Cartoon Network. *The Accidental Prime Minister* was his debut children's novel. Check out Tom's website for more information on the *Accidental* series.

Tom lives in Devon and his hobbies include drinking tea, looking out of the window, and biscuits. His hates include spiders and running out of tea and biscuits.

tommclaughlin.co.uk

# ALSO BY Tom McLaughlin